FROM THE
NANCY DREW FILES

THE CASE: An unwelcome act of revenge crashes Wendy Harriman's high school reunion party.

CONTACT: Nancy is Wendy's old schoolmate—but there's plenty she never knew about the popular cheerleader.

SUSPECTS: Celia Quaid—she never forgot Wendy's cruel taunts about her weight problem.

Monica Beckwith—the actress hates Wendy for stealing the stage during a class play—and stealing her boyfriend as well.

Judd Reese—the former greaser always resented being snubbed by Wendy.

COMPLICATIONS: Nancy's former boyfriend, Don Cameron, would like to rekindle their romance—which makes Ned hot under the collar!

Books in THE NANCY DREW FILES® Series

Available from ARCHWAY paperbacks

THE NANCY DREW FILES™ CASE • 27

MOST LIKELY
TO DIE

Carolyn Keene

AN ARCHWAY PAPERBACK
Published by POCKET BOOKS
New York   London   Toronto   Sydney   Tokyo

AN ARCHWAY PAPERBACK *Original*

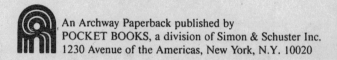

An Archway Paperback published by
POCKET BOOKS, a division of Simon & Schuster Inc.
1230 Avenue of the Americas, New York, N.Y. 10020

ISBN: 0-671-64694-X

First Archway Paperback printing September 1988

10 9 8 7 6 5 4 3 2 1

NANCY DREW, AN ARCHWAY PAPERBACK and colophon
are registered trademarks of Simon & Schuster Inc.

THE NANCY DREW FILES is a trademark
of Simon & Schuster Inc.

Printed in the U.S.A.

IL 7+

Chapter

One

OKAY, BESS. YOU have exactly three minutes," Nancy Drew said firmly, glancing at her watch. "If you're not ready by then, we're leaving without you."

"But, Nancy, I've got to look *perfect!*" wailed Bess Marvin. She was staring anxiously at herself in her new bikini in the full-length mirror in Nancy's room. She pushed a stray lock of blond hair back into place. "I can't believe you and George are so calm. I mean, here we are about to see everyone from high school for the first time in ages—and you're not even worried? *I* won't be happy at this party unless every single guy there says how gorgeous I've gotten since high school."

1

"But it hasn't been that long!" said George Fayne, Bess's first cousin. "You look the same, Bess. Gorgeous! Now, please, let's go!"

Quickly Bess stepped into a pair of white baggy pants and pulled a turquoise- and white-striped T-shirt over her head.

"Hey, up there! Don't you think we'd better leave?" called a voice from the living room downstairs.

"We're on our way, Ned!" Nancy called to her boyfriend, Ned Nickerson. "Let me make sure I've got the invitation so we'll know how to get there," she added as the three girls started downstairs. "Oh, yes, here it is. And here we are, Ned," she added as Bess joined them and walked into the living room. "Sorry to keep you waiting."

The invitation that had thrown Bess into such a panic was from Wendy Harriman, who'd been in their class at River Heights High School.

"End-of-summer beach party for the best class ever!" it said in bright pink letters. "Be there at 4:00 P.M. to party with all your old friends from River Heights High. Come on, gang—let's make Wednesday night a winner!" Obviously Wendy hadn't forgotten her pep-rally techniques—she had been head cheerleader. The wording of the invitation sounded exactly the way she always talked.

The party was going to be held at Wendy's parents' cottage on Sprucewood Lake. Nancy had never been there, even though she'd been fairly friendly with Wendy in high school. At least Nancy had been one of the people Wendy was nice to sometimes.

Nancy hadn't seen Wendy since the day they'd graduated, but when she had called Wendy to accept the invitation, Wendy sounded as perky and bubbly as ever. "It'll be a mini-reunion!" she had promised. "And feel free to bring Ned. He's practically a member of our class anyway."

Ned had graduated from a different school from Nancy and her friends, but Wendy was right. Nancy and Ned had met while she was on a case, and they'd been going together ever since.

Nancy could hardly stand the thought that he had to return to Emerson College right after Labor Day. She was glad they'd have one last party to mark the end of their happy summer together.

"Do you think we could go together? In the same car?" Bess asked in a plaintive voice. "It would be more fun to get there with some—you know—moral support."

Nancy glanced over at Ned. She knew he'd been counting on taking her alone, but he was grinning broadly.

"How could we deprive you of our moral support, Bess?" he said. "We'll go in my car."

"The scenery is gorgeous," Nancy commented after they'd left the city behind and were winding around Sprucewood Lake. "And look at these houses. They're practically mansions!"

In the back seat, Bess sighed. "I guess that's just the way it goes. Why shouldn't the girl who has everything have the perfect beach house, too?"

"What's the matter, Bess?" Nancy asked gently. "You don't sound like yourself today."

Bess was silent for a minute. "I guess it's just that the idea of seeing Wendy Harriman makes me nervous," she said at last. "It probably doesn't bother you, Nan—you're so confident. But there's just something about Wendy—I know she's nice and everything. But when we were in high school she made me feel like a total clod. She was always so perfect! Perfect nails! Perfect hair! Perfect body! And going back to see her *and* everyone from our class is making me feel like a clod all over again."

"I know what you mean," said George. "It wasn't anything she actually said, but Wendy always made me feel as though being athletic was weird. I got the feeling she couldn't really accept anyone who wasn't exactly like her."

"She *was* kind of catty sometimes, but she was

4

probably just insecure," Nancy said. "I'm sure she's gotten over it by now."

"What's she doing these days, anyway?" asked Ned. "Is she going to college?"

"Sort of," Nancy answered. "She said she was working part-time at a stationery store and taking some classes."

"Doesn't sound too strenuous," observed George.

"We must be getting close to the house," Ned said. "What did you say the number was, Nancy? Never mind. That's got to be it."

Ahead of them was a rambling old beach house whose front yard was packed solid with cars.

"Hi, Nancy!" Wendy Harriman shrieked, bouncing over to the car as they drove up. "Hi, Ned! Hi, Bess! Hi, George!"

"Let's go home," whispered Bess dourly. But everyone else in the car was getting out.

Wendy had always been one of the cutest girls in the class. "A walking cola commercial," Ned had once said. With beautiful auburn hair, freckles, and sparkling green eyes, she had managed to stand out.

"I was beginning to think you guys weren't coming!" Wendy chirped now. "Everyone else is here"—she pouted a little—"except my boyfriend, Rod. I really wanted people to meet him, but he's out of town. Anyway, it's great to see you. Bess, you haven't changed a bit. You look

5

exactly the same. And what about you, George— are you still a jock?"

"I guess *you'd* say so," George said. Her smile was a little stiff, but Wendy didn't see it. She had already turned to Ned.

"You're looking pretty healthy, Mr. Nickerson," she said merrily.

Ned smiled. "I try."

"That's good. You know, you've got some competition tonight—Don Cameron's looking better than ever! Oh, there's Marcy Meyer! Hey, *Marce!*" Wendy dashed up to a car that was just pulling into the driveway.

For a second the four of them just stood watching her. "She hasn't changed at all," George said at last. "Except maybe she's even perkier. Has anyone ever *died* of 'perky'?" Bess laughed. "The water looks great, anyway. I'm going in."

"I'll come, too," Bess said.

"I wonder what Wendy meant by competition," Ned said to Nancy.

"I have no idea," said Nancy. She squeezed his hand. "Let's go talk to some of the other kids."

A volleyball game was in progress on the lush side lawn, and Nancy and Ned headed in that direction. Very few kids were actually playing the game. Most of them were sitting or standing and listening to a handsome black-haired boy.

"Patrick Emmons!" Nancy said.

If Wendy had been the most popular girl in the class, Patrick had definitely been the most popular boy. As a matter of fact, those two had gone steady through most of high school. They were the perfect couple, and even when they'd broken up in the middle of their senior year they managed to stay good friends.

It wasn't just that Patrick was so good-looking —it was that he shone at everything he did. He'd been the captain of the football team and president of the student council. He'd done lots of volunteer work without being a goody-goody about it. And no one was surprised when he had won a full scholarship to an Ivy League college in the East.

Now he was talking animatedly, his back to the volleyball net. "So then my fraternity decided we had to get even. I wired the dean's office for sound, and when he— Nancy! Ned! How are you?" he broke off to say.

"Just great," Nancy said as she and Ned moved in beside him. "How's college?"

Patrick smiled. "Unbelievable. I'm having the best time of my life."

"Still playing football?" Ned asked. Ned was a top athlete himself, and he knew Patrick had played on just about every varsity team at River Heights High.

"Is he still playing football!" exclaimed a pudgy girl named Lori Blum. Nancy remem-

7

bered that Lori had always had a crush on Patrick. "He's only the first freshman in twenty years at that school to make varsity."

Patrick was blushing. "I just got lucky. I only hope I can keep my grades up at the same time."

"I wouldn't worry too much," said Lori. "Nancy, he also won the freshman composition prize *and* the history prize. But you won't get him to talk about that. You have to drag it out of him."

"Well, I'm impressed," Nancy said. "Your parents must be, too." Patrick had been the first person in his family to go to college.

"I—I guess they are." Patrick ducked his head. "They gave me a car." He pointed to a sleek black Corvette. "But really, I don't want to talk about myself. What have you been doing, Nancy? Still sleuthing?"

Before Nancy could answer, she heard a familiar voice behind her. "Any room over there?"

She turned to see Monica Beckwith looking down at the group. Monica had been the class's star actress—so good that she had started getting parts in a regional theater even before graduating. Now she was doing TV commercials for a cosmetics company based in New York, and Nancy was sure it wouldn't be long before she hit the big time.

Standing beside Monica, half hidden by her, was a girl Nancy had never seen before. If

Monica was glamorous—an ash blonde with deep violet eyes—this girl was a genuine beauty. Her long black hair fell sleekly down her back, and her smoky gray eyes were fringed with the longest lashes Nancy had ever seen. But why did she look so sullen?

"Of course there's room, Monica," Nancy said warmly. "And for your friend, too." She smiled at the girl beside Monica. "I'm sorry, I don't know your name, but—"

"Celia Quaid."

"Celia Quaid!"

Nancy couldn't help gasping. She would never have recognized this beautiful girl as Celia!

"You've lost so much weight!" Lori Blum said.

"Sixty pounds," Celia said curtly.

"That's fantastic!" said Nancy. "You look wonderful!"

But Celia wasn't smiling. "Thanks."

Monica had already sat down on the grass next to Nancy. "Wouldn't you like to sit down, too?" she asked Celia.

"Not right now." Celia turned to walk away and almost bumped into Wendy Harriman.

"Hi, gang! Doesn't Celia look great?" Wendy said. "I still can't believe it. How'd you ever do it, Celia?"

Celia stared at Wendy for a second, and it wasn't a pleasant stare. "You should know" was

9

all she said. "I'm going swimming." And she walked away.

"Well! What's the matter with *her?*" asked Wendy, tossing back her hair petulantly.

"Maybe she's a little self-conscious or something," said Ned.

But if it made Celia self-conscious to be congratulated on her amazing achievement, why had she come to the party?

Whatever the reason, the scene she had just witnessed made Nancy uncomfortable. "Want to go for a swim, too?" she asked Ned.

"Sure," he answered, jumping to his feet and grabbing her outstretched hand.

But they never got to the lake. Don Cameron was moving toward them, a delighted look on his face. And when she saw him, Nancy knew what Wendy had meant by "competition."

Don had been Nancy's boyfriend before she started going with Ned. Like Ned and Patrick, he had also been a star athlete. He was a perfectly nice guy, but Nancy had never managed to feel starry-eyed and romantic about him. That was why she'd broken up with him.

Still, Don had been a lot of fun, even if he didn't make her heart beat fast. "Hi, Don!" Nancy said enthusiastically.

Don's eyes were glowing. Before Nancy knew it, he'd taken her hand and kissed her on the cheek. "It's great to see you again!" he said. "How's it going?"

"Just fine. You remember Ned?" Nancy asked, determined to remind him how things stood.

"Of course," Don said. Ned smiled and shook his hand. A little of the light faded from Don's face.

Nancy decided not to draw things out any longer. "Bess! George!" she called, waving to them on the beach. "Come over and say hi to Don!"

Bess and George sized up the situation at a glance. Chattering and giggling, they drew Don away with them toward the water.

Nancy looked up at Ned, who was staring after Don. "You're not jealous," she said, grinning at him.

"No," Ned said slowly. "I was just thinking about how lucky I am." Bending his head, he lightly kissed Nancy on her other cheek. When he drew back, he winked. "Now you have a matched set."

A roar from a motorcycle drew their attention just then.

"It's Judd Reese!" Nancy said. "He's sure cleaned up his act."

Judd had been the biggest greaser in their class—scruffy, leather-jacketed, and surly. He was still wearing a leather jacket that day, but every trace of scruffiness was gone. Judd looked lean and elegant—a gentleman biker. "Isn't that a pretty expensive machine?" Nancy asked Ned.

"Top of the line," he answered.

"I wonder what *he's* been doing since we graduated," Nancy said.

"What's he doing here?" Wendy hissed angrily, coming up at Nancy's side. "I didn't invite *him!*"

Judd had swung off his motorcycle and was striding toward them. "Hey, Wendy," he said. "Heard you were having a little party, so I decided to stop by."

Wendy looked furious—and a little scared. "Fine," she said, controlling the tremor in her voice. "As long as none of your friends are coming with you."

"Don't worry," said Judd. "I don't have those friends anymore. Your house won't get trashed today—at least not by me!" He grinned. "Where can I get something to drink?"

"There's soda in those ice coolers over there." Wendy pointed to the picnic table.

"Thanks."

"What should I do?" Wendy moaned as she watched Judd saunter away. "What if he gets nasty?"

"Why should he?" Nancy asked.

"Well, you know what he was like in school!"

"It looks as though he's changed since then. I

wouldn't worry about it. Look, is there anything I can do to help with the food?"

"Good idea." Wendy's brow cleared. "Let's bring the burgers out to the grill."

When they'd brought out the trays, Wendy climbed onto a picnic bench and clapped her hands. "Okay, gang!" she shouted. "Burger time! Who's going to light the fire?"

"Me," said Patrick, stepping up to the grill. "Where's the charcoal starter, Wendy?"

"I don't see it anywh— Oh, here it is." Wendy reached in back of the grill to hand it to him.

Patrick bent over the grill and carefully squeezed the plastic container. He struck a kitchen match against its box and tossed it into the charcoal. Then he screamed.

An explosion of flame leaped out of the grill— right onto his shirt and face!

Chapter

Two

NANCY SNATCHED UP a crumpled beach towel lying on the grass beside the grill. Pressing the damp terrycloth against Patrick's face and shirt, she smothered the flames instantly. A few people in the crowd didn't even realize what had happened.

But the flames on the grill were still blazing furiously, soaring high into the air. Nancy grabbed a pitcher of lemonade and flung it onto the fire. Ned grabbed two more pitchers and did the same. In a second the fire had died out, and all that was left in the grill was a hissing mess of soggy coals.

"Sorry about the lemonade, Wendy," Nancy said. "Patrick, let me see your face. Are you okay?"

Patrick was still patting the damp towel against his skin. His shirt was singed, and so was his hair. His face had been reddened by the heat —but there were no bad burns that Nancy could see.

"I—I think I'm okay," he said, sounding dazed. "Thanks to you, Nancy."

"Well, your skin's not broken anywhere, so I don't think you need a doctor. But you'd better put some ice on your face," Nancy said. "Could someone please—"

George, who had come out of the water, was already filling one of the empty pitchers with ice from the coolers of soda cans. She handed it to Patrick.

"Thanks, George. And, Wendy, if you've got some plastic bags in the kitchen, we can improvise some ice bags for him."

"Sure. Come on, Patrick. Let's go get you fixed up," said Wendy, leading Patrick into the kitchen.

"And now," said Nancy grimly, "I want to take a look at that charcoal starter." She picked up the plastic bottle and sniffed it.

"Just what I thought," she said. "Gasoline."

There was a murmur from the kids gathered

around her. "But the bottle says it's charcoal starter," Ned protested.

"The same thing could have happened to any of us," Nancy said.

"But I don't understand," said Bess. "Why would anybody put gasoline into that container?"

"If you wanted to play a trick on someone . . ." Nancy said, leaving the sentence unfinished. A really horrible trick, she thought.

It was the only explanation she could come up with. Someone must have substituted gasoline for the starter fluid on purpose. But who would have done a thing like that—and why? Nancy could hardly believe her own suspicions.

"Well," she said out loud, "I bet it was the only bottle someone could find to put the gasoline in. Accidents can happen. Ned, how about giving me a hand getting rid of these wet coals? We can get the grill all ready, and someone can go buy us some real charcoal starter."

"I'll go," said someone from the back of the crowd.

"Perfect," Nancy said gratefully. "Now we're back on track!"

Wendy came out of the house a few minutes later. "Patrick's just getting cleaned up, and then he'll be right out," she reported.

When Patrick did come out, Nancy was relieved to see that he looked fine. Only the front of his shirt—which was blackened—hinted that anything had happened to him.

"Boy, Nancy," he said, "I guess that'll teach me not to put so much starter on next time!"

"Right," Nancy said with a laugh. Patrick hadn't heard that it was gasoline in the bottle, and Nancy decided not to scare him after the shock he had just had.

"Come with me while I change, Bess," she said. "All of a sudden I'm dying for a swim. Ned, how about you?"

"I think I'll hang out and man the grill when the starter fluid gets here," Ned answered. "I've gotten a lot better at it, you know." Bess and Nancy both grinned. They could both remember a time when Ned's barbecuing skills had consisted mainly of torching the main course.

"By the time you're finished with your swim, I'll have a perfect hamburger all ready for you," Ned continued.

"Well, watch out!" Nancy warned him. "We don't want *you* catching on fire, too."

"Don't worry," said Patrick. "I'll be standing right beside him to make sure he doesn't do anything wrong."

"Try not to burn the burgers," Bess called back over her shoulder.

17

"You have no faith," Ned answered.

"It has nothing to do with faith—I've *eaten* your hamburgers," said Bess, and she ran for the house.

"Why'd you poke me earlier, Nancy?" Bess whispered as they stopped before entering the house. "Why didn't you want Patrick to know there was gasoline in that container?"

Nancy explained. "I'm sure—or I'm hoping, anyway—that there was just some kind of mistake. No sense getting Patrick upset when we can't prove anything. Can you believe this house?" she added, changing the subject. "They certainly are prepared for parties!"

Bess and she had entered a huge dressing room on the first floor. A mirror—complete with makeup lights—covered one entire wall. There was a mahogany wardrobe filled with brass clothes hangers against another wall, and a blue-flowered chintz chaise longue stood ready for any guest who might feel like lying down. On a table under the window was a huge stack of fluffy beach towels, and next to them were all kinds of suntan lotions and sunscreens.

"It's better than a hotel," Bess agreed. Then she lowered her voice. "I only wish Wendy was being a little—a little nicer. Every time she's passed me she's said something catty! I thought people were supposed to get sweeter once they graduated from high school."

"I couldn't agree with you more," said someone behind them.

Nancy and Bess wheeled around—and there was Celia Quaid.

"Celia!" said Bess. "Uh, hi! Did you—um—have you been in here long?"

"I heard everything you said about Wendy, if that's what you mean," said Celia. She strolled calmly over to the mirror and began brushing her hair.

"Shhhhh!" said Bess frantically. "Please forget I said that. It was so rude of me—and in Wendy's house, too. I didn't really mean it."

"Don't worry," said Celia. "I won't say anything. People like that always end up getting what they deserve, anyway." Without a backward glance at either Nancy or Bess, she put her brush back into her beach bag and walked out of the room.

Bess sighed. "Open mouth, insert foot. You ready for that swim now? I need to cool off my red face."

Nancy tightened the ties on her bikini and picked up a towel. "Let's go," she said.

People were streaming in and out of the house. Nancy and Bess threaded their way through the crowd and headed down the lawn to the lake.

"Hi, George!" Nancy called happily when she saw George's head bob up next to the dock.

Then her heart sank. Don Cameron was out there, too. He spotted her right away and came splashing out of the water toward her.

"The water's fantastic!" he said. "Come on in!"

Nancy glanced around for Bess—but Bess had melted out of sight. Oh, no! Nancy thought. This is one time I *need* a chaperon!

"I'm afraid I won't be much fun, Don," she said quietly. "I just want to do a few laps before I help Ned with the food."

"I see," said Don. Then there was an awkward pause. "I guess I'll go in and change, then," he said.

The water *was* fantastic, but Nancy wasn't in the mood to appreciate it anymore. She just slowly swam up to George. "I guess Don doesn't feel like being ignored," she said bleakly.

George smiled sympathetically. "There was no way I could head him off," she said. "I tried, believe me."

"Well, you and Bess did a great job of distracting him earlier. Oh, well, after tonight I won't have to see him anymore."

"That's right. I'll race you to the dock!" George suddenly shouted, and she plunged forward into the water.

After a few minutes of hard swimming, Nancy

felt better. She emerged from the lake feeling much more cheerful than when she had gone in.

"Nancy! George! Come here and look at these when you've changed!" Bess called. "Someone brought a bunch of old yearbooks!"

The two girls rushed in to change, then grabbed hamburgers from the tray and hurried over to a bunch of kids sitting on the side lawn. "Look, this one's from ninth grade. Can you believe my *hair* back then?" squealed Bess.

"Look at George, too," Wendy said. "What a bean pole you were, George."

"I sure was," George agreed amiably. "Not you, though, Wendy. Even back then you looked like the perfect cheerleader."

Wendy darted a suspicious glance at George, but George was staring innocently back at her.

"You look pretty much the same as you did when you were a freshman, Nancy," Wendy said quickly.

"Yes," Ned agreed. "I would have gone out with you back then if I'd known you."

"That's good to hear," Nancy said, gazing fondly at him. "I remember that necklace, Wendy," she added, pointing to another picture. "I always loved it. Do you still have it?"

"What do you mean? I'm wearing it—" Wendy stopped. "I mean, I was wearing it. I put it on just before the party. Or did I?" She looked puzzled. "Maybe I meant to put it on and left it

21

in my room. I'd better go check." She hurried back to the house.

"These hamburgers are great, Ned. I apologize for my rude crack," Bess said around a mouthful of rare meat and bun.

"Thanks. Patrick and I—"

He never finished. There was a sudden terrified scream from the house, and Wendy's sheet-white face appeared at an upstairs window.

"Somebody come up here!" she called. "My— my room. It's—"

Nancy was already tearing toward the house, Ned, Bess, and George trailing her.

They raced up the stairs—and stopped in the doorway to Wendy's room, shocked by the scene before them.

Wendy's room had been completely trashed. All her bureau drawers had been pulled out and their contents dumped on the floor. Her jewelry box lay on the floor, too, empty except for a few trinkets. Her makeup and perfume had been smeared all over her dressing table, and her mirror was cracked all the way across.

But that wasn't why Wendy was screaming.

On her bed lay a doll—a doll dressed in a cheerleader's costume, with a large butcher knife through its chest.

The knife was pinning down a piece of paper.

Nancy stepped forward and pulled the knife out so she could read the message.

It was made up from letters cut out of newspaper headlines. Nancy read out loud, "'Greetings to the most self-centered brat at River Heights High. Wish this doll were you!'"

Chapter
Three

"ALL RIGHT, WENDY, you're going to be fine," Nancy said soothingly for what seemed like the hundredth time. "The police are on their way. In fact, I think I hear them now." She peered out through Wendy's window. "Here they are."

"They're up there, officers," came the sound of Patrick's voice on the stairs. In a second his anxious face peered into Wendy's room. "Wendy, here are Officer Risdale"—he gestured toward the younger of the two men—"and Officer Marsh. Are you feeling better?"

His question only triggered a new flood of

tears. "I'm okay, but what about my *stuff?*" Wendy wailed. "What are my parents going to say when I tell them everything's gone?"

"They'll know it wasn't your fault," Nancy said, reassuring her. She smiled at the two officers, who were standing awkwardly in the doorway. "I'm Nancy Drew," she said, "and this is Wendy Harriman." Quickly she told them what had happened.

"What exactly has been taken?" Officer Risdale asked.

"My—my cassette player." Wendy's voice quavered. "And my miniature watch–TV that my father gave me last Christmas, and just about all of my jewelry. There was a diamond bracelet that belonged to my grandmother—" Her eyes filled with tears again. "I spent most of the summer out here, so I wanted my stuff with me. Why didn't I leave it back in River Heights?"

"Has anyone at the party had the chance to get up here?" said Risdale.

Wendy looked bewildered. "Everyone, I guess. I mean, people changed into their suits in the house, and there were lots of kids going into the kitchen. There've been people in and out the whole time the party's been going on."

"I'd hope that this was done by a guest at the party," put in Officer Marsh. "But we just have to check every possibility. I wonder if you could wait outside for a few minutes so we can go through things here? We'll be down in a little while."

Wendy moved obediently to the door. Nancy lagged behind. "You should know about one other thing that happened here earlier," she began. "When we were getting ready to barbecue—"

"Please wait downstairs with the others, miss," said Officer Marsh firmly. "We'll be just a few minutes."

Nancy stifled a sigh of frustration before following Wendy downstairs.

Risdale and Marsh came down very soon after that—too soon, Nancy thought, for them to have investigated the room thoroughly.

Wendy jumped to her feet when she saw them. "Who did it? Do you know?" she asked eagerly.

Officer Risdale gave her a patient smile. "I'm afraid not. It does look like a clear case of breaking and entering, though. We'll *try* to recover the stolen items, but I can't promise anything."

"Breaking and entering?" Nancy asked incredulously. "What kind of evidence do you have?"

Risdale obviously hadn't heard of Nancy, and he spoke to her as if she were a child. "There are marks on the ground outside the window that look like they were made by a ladder. The window appears to have been forced from the outside, and there are traces of makeup on the windowsill. We can't tell for sure without analyzing them, but there's no reason not to think they're from one of the spilled bottles on the dressing table. There are no traces of makeup or powder leading out of the room. The perpetrator probably exited through the window also. Now, if there are no further questions, young lady, we'll be on our way." He said it as a slight rebuke to Nancy.

"But what about the doll and the note?" she asked, ignoring the man's attitude. "Doesn't that point to someone at the party having committed the burglary?"

"There's not necessarily any connection," said Officer Marsh. "It's probably not relevant to the burglary."

"But what about the charcoal starter fluid?" Nancy filled the men in on what had happened to Patrick earlier.

Officer Marsh didn't seem impressed. "Possibly someone put gasoline into an empty starter bottle to kill poison ivy. We see that kind of thing all the time out here."

"We don't *have* any poison ivy at this house!" Wendy protested hotly.

"You'd be surprised," said Officer Marsh. "It's all over the place. Look, we'll be in touch. Where are your parents, by the way?"

"Back in River Heights," said Wendy.

"Well, why don't you have them give us a call tomorrow? And, as I said, we'll be in touch as soon as possible."

"They treated me as though I was about two years old!" Wendy burst out as soon as the police car was out of sight.

"They *were* patronizing," Nancy said. "Look, Wendy, if you don't mind, I'd like to do a little investigating myself. I just don't think this robbery was an outside job."

"I'd feel much better knowing you were working on the case, too," said Wendy. "You might as well start tonight," she added ruefully. "It looks as though the party's over. So much for school spirit."

Nancy looked around. It was true. What had just happened had managed to derail the party pretty thoroughly. Most of the guests were standing around in awkward little groups, and some of them were starting to drift off to their cars.

"Well, there's still time to talk to a few people, at least," Nancy said. "Bess, George, why don't you sort of hang out around the cars. Look in them to see if you notice anything weird stashed inside. It's hard to believe anyone would be dumb enough to hide stolen goods right here, but we'd better check everything we can."

"What do you want me to do?" Wendy asked.

Nancy smiled. "Just go back to being hostess. I'll tell you about anything I turn up."

Not that I'm likely to turn anything up, she said to herself a little later. No one she'd talked to had noticed anything odd going on.

Nancy asked Ned to check out the ground under Wendy's window and the ladder. Ned found a ladder in the gardening shed, but he couldn't tell if it had been used for the robbery. It was tall enough to reach the window, but there was no dirt on the legs, no sign that it had been used.

While he was occupied Nancy talked to the guests, and she did learn something interesting from Monica Beckwith.

"I don't want to seem like a tattletale," Monica had said conspiratorially. "And this may not have anything to do with anything. But back in school, Wendy once caught Celia Quaid putting a poison-pen note into her locker. I don't remember exactly what the note said, but I *do* remember that it was sort of like the one in Wendy's room tonight."

"I wonder why Wendy didn't mention that to me," said Nancy thoughtfully.

"Maybe she was embarrassed to," Monica said. "She really laced into Celia when she caught her. It was kind of awful to watch. By the time she was done with her, Celia was sobbing. She didn't come to school for about a week after that—I know because she was in my homeroom."

"I guess I'd better talk to Celia," said Nancy. "Do you know where she is?"

"Gone," said Monica. "She left a while ago— just about the time the police got here."

That certainly didn't look innocent. And Nancy was remembering Celia's strange remark in the dressing room. "People like that usually get what they deserve," she'd said. Had Celia made sure Wendy would get what she deserved?

One thing was sure. Wendy wasn't always the bouncy, sweet girl she tried to be. It looked as though she had had a few enemies—and Celia had definitely been one of them.

Well, my brand-new number one suspect isn't around for questioning, Nancy thought. I might as well go home, too. It's getting late, and we have a long drive ahead of us. The next morning will be soon enough to start the investigation properly.

"Thanks for telling me this, Monica," she said. "And I'd appreciate it if you didn't mention it to anyone else."

"No problem," Monica answered.

Nancy went to round up Bess and George, who reported that they hadn't found anything suspicious. Then she found Ned and said goodbye to Wendy.

"What did you find out?" Wendy asked.

"Not much, really," said Nancy cautiously. "Just odds and ends." She didn't want to make Wendy suspicious of Celia without more facts to go on. "I'll call you tomorrow," she promised. "And in the meantime, don't touch anything in your room. I'll check it out better tomorrow."

As Nancy, Ned, Bess, and George were walking toward the car, Bess suddenly stopped. "Our suits!" she said. "We left them inside! Let's go get them, George."

"I'd better make sure the fire in the grill's really out," said Ned. "I was the last person using it."

Ned's car was parked off to the left—standing alone now. Nancy was moving down a moonlit path toward it when Don Cameron suddenly loomed out of the shadows in front of her.

"Don! You scared me!" Nancy exclaimed.

"I'm sorry. I didn't mean to. I just wanted to catch you alone. I'd really like to talk to you, Nancy. Can I give you a lift home?"

How many times do I have to explain this? Nancy wondered. Aloud she said, "Thanks, Don, but Ned is driving me."

"Oh. I should have figured. Well—what I wanted to say is—stay away from this case, Nancy. You might get in over your head."

For a second Nancy was so startled she couldn't answer. Was Don threatening her? It certainly sounded that way. But if he'd been the one who broke into Wendy's room, why would he drop hints about it?

"Don't worry about me, Don," Nancy finally managed to say.

"I can't help it. Anyone who'd do something like that to a doll is sick. I don't think you should get involved."

"Look, Don, I appreciate your being worried about me"—even though I wish you'd stop, she added to herself—"but I can handle it. Really."

Don took a step closer. "Nancy, don't you see that I'm trying to tell you—"

"Tell her what, Don?"

"Ned!" Nancy gasped. Ned was standing right in back of Don, and he wasn't smiling. "Don's been trying to give me some advice about the case."

"Don't worry, Ned," said Don with a mirthless laugh. "She won't listen to me, anyway. Good night, Nancy—Ned." And he walked off into the heavy darkness under some trees.

"He just came out of nowhere," Nancy said, explaining to Ned.

Ned gave her a quick hug. "He's still hung up on you—and I can't blame him. I'm just glad we're not in high school anymore. I'd hate to think of you running into him every day," he said, his arm around her waist as they made their way to his car.

"That's exactly how I feel," said Nancy. "Here

come Bess and George." She reached out and opened the car door on her side.

What was that strange buzzing sound? She poked her head in the car. And what was that white mass on the driver's seat? Puzzled, Nancy leaned in farther to see.

Then she screamed—which was her mistake. The object was a hornet's nest, and Nancy had woken the insects up. Before she could slam the car door, they poured out of the nest straight at her. In another second she'd be covered with welts from head to toe!

Chapter

Four

Ned! GET BACK!" Nancy shouted, scrambling over the hood of Ned's car and grabbing his hand. The two of them dashed toward Bess and George and stopped about thirty feet from the car.

When Nancy and Ned turned, they saw that the hornets were still swarming out of the open car door. But once they had been evicted from their hive and were out in the air, the insects seemed to lose their sense of purpose and flew off in all directions. Soon there were only a few tired-looking creatures crawling slowly over the surface of the car.

"Well! I guess the worst is over. The hive's still in there, though," Nancy said to Ned.

"We'd better get it out. There may be some hornets still inside," Ned said.

He looked around and found a long stick lying under the trees. "Maybe we can just poke the nest out with this."

"I'll stay here and watch," said Bess with a shudder. "I don't want to be there if any more of those guys come flying out. What if that was just the first installment?

"Call me when you're done," she added as Nancy, Ned, and George walked toward the car.

Nancy peeked into the car from Ned's side. The papery gray nest certainly seemed quiet enough. No hornets flew out when she opened Ned's door.

Ned jabbed the stick into the hive and carried it off into the trees. No hornets flew out.

"Okay, Bess. All clear," Nancy called.

Bess walked slowly up to them. Standing well away from the car, she leaned forward and peered into the front seat. "You're right," she said, relieved. "Let's get out of here. I've had enough partying tonight."

The four of them climbed carefully into the car, and as Ned was turning the car around Nancy noticed a piece of paper lying on the floor at her feet. She picked it up.

Like the note in Wendy's room, the words had been cut from newspaper headlines. Nancy's breath quickened as she read out loud. "'Still a snoop, aren't you? Don't stir things up—or this is only the beginning!'"

Ned pulled over to the side of the road and looked at the piece of paper. Then he passed it to Bess and George in the back seat.

"Oh, no!" Bess gasped. "Someone's out to get you, too!"

"Obviously," Nancy said. "But this note seems like overkill. Didn't they think the nest would be enough?"

"Well, someone's trying to stop you from investigating—as usual," Ned said. He started the car again. "I don't suppose it'll work."

"Of course not," Nancy answered, her lips a tight line. She was already trying to figure out what this note—and the nest—had to do with what had happened earlier in the evening.

"'*Still* a snoop,'" she said aloud. "Do you guys remember that people used to call me Nancy the Snoop back in high school?"

"Yeah," George said. "When you first decided you wanted to be a detective. But they were just joking then. This isn't a joke, Nancy. Not really."

Not any more than the stabbed doll or the gasoline had been. Nancy didn't like being on the receiving end of a prank like this, but she was glad of one thing: The note and the hornet's nest were evidence that the culprit she was looking for was probably a guest at the party.

"I wish you didn't have to start a new case without either me or Hannah around," said Nancy's father in a worried voice the next morning. "Why couldn't this have happened next week?"

Carson Drew was an internationally successful lawyer, and he spent a lot of time out of town. Usually the Drews' housekeeper, Hannah Gruen —who was almost like a mother to Nancy—was there to keep her company when her father was away. But an old friend of Hannah's had broken her hip a few days earlier, and Hannah had flown to Buffalo, New York, to take care of her.

"Now, Dad, you know I take very good care of myself." Nancy grinned at him across the breakfast table as she jumped up to clear her dishes. "Besides, this is just high school prank stuff. Nothing to worry about, really. Now, do you need help with anything before I head over to Wendy's? Are you all packed?"

Carson Drew's face relaxed into a smile. "You just take care of yourself," he said. "Don't worry about me. I think I'll be able to pack my own suitcase—even without Hannah here."

* * *

Before she had gone to bed the night before, Nancy decided to speak to Wendy Harriman first thing in the morning. She arranged to meet Wendy at eight o'clock at her house in River Heights.

When Nancy got there, Wendy was still in her bathrobe, with her hair tousled and no makeup on. "Sorry," she murmured, yawning wide. "I meant to get dressed, but I'm still so tired from last night— Anyway, come in. We'll go to the kitchen."

The beach house had been beautiful, but the house in town was unbelievable. Perfectly decorated and impeccably clean, it looked as though it had been made ready for a magazine spread. Even the kitchen was like a stage set and not exactly homey.

Wendy poured them both some orange juice and drained half of hers before asking, "Well, what do we do?"

"First of all, whoever's after you tried to scare me off the case last night." Quickly Nancy told Wendy about the hornet's nest and the note. "I want you to be careful," she finished. "In a way, these pranks worry me more than the fact that your jewelry was stolen. Robbery's pretty straightforward, but there's something twisted about all these pranks. Do you have any idea if someone in our class has it in for you?"

Wendy's green eyes were wide. "Of course not!" she said. "Why? I mean, lots of people were jealous of me." She shrugged as if to indicate she knew Nancy could understand that. "But I don't know anyone who didn't like me."

"You mentioned something last night about your boyfriend being out of town."

"Rod? But he'd never do anything like this, even for a joke. Anyway, he really is out of town. He's doing a show in Philadelphia."

"Oh? Is he an actor?"

Suddenly Wendy looked a little uncomfortable. "Yes, he is," she said shortly.

Well, whoever he was, Rod definitely wasn't a suspect. But what about Celia? "I was wondering how well you knew Celia Quaid," Nancy began.

Wendy's face hardened. "What has she been telling you? All right, I admit I wasn't the nicest to her in high school, but she deserved it. You remember what she looked like back then. It drives me crazy when people don't even try to get in shape!"

Nancy didn't answer. She couldn't think of anything to say to an insensitive remark like that.

"Anyway, why do you think somebody wants to get *me?*" Wendy asked. "I mean, look at that little trick with the charcoal starter. Whoever put the gas in there couldn't be sure who'd get zapped."

"That's true," said Nancy. "It's possible that the culprit is after more than one person."

"Well, if Celia did it, the joke's on her. She's always been in love with Patrick."

"I didn't know that," said Nancy, startled. "Did she *tell* you that?"

"She didn't have to. Back in school it was obvious. You should have seen her face when she'd pass him in the halls. I used to tease him that he should go with her. I said she'd be a lot nicer to him than I was. That was before she got so gorgeous, of course."

"Was that before or after you broke up with him?"

"I didn't break up with Patrick!" Wendy exclaimed, slightly red-faced. "He broke up with me—in the middle of senior year. I was pretty upset for a while, but we did stay friends. And it was just as well we broke up, anyway. It's hard to stay together when you're at different colleges."

"I guess that depends," said Nancy. She was thinking of Ned. "Well, thanks for talking to me, Wendy. Give me a call if anything occurs to you—any reason someone might think of you as an enemy. Where are your parents, by the way?" she added.

Wendy's face grew red again. "Well, actually, they're in Europe. I didn't tell the police that. I didn't want them to think I'm the kind of person who rushes out to have a party the minute her parents leave town."

"I understand," said Nancy. But she felt uneasy. She wasn't sure Wendy could handle any problems that might come up. "Well, I'll talk to you soon."

It turned out to be a lot sooner than she'd expected. Nancy had only been home for a few minutes when she heard brakes screech in the driveway, a car door slam, and feet pound up to her front door. "Nancy!" Wendy screamed. "Let me in!"

Nancy opened the door—and Wendy almost fell into her arms.

"Look at this! Look at this!" she said, practically babbling. "Someone delivered it to our house right after you left. I was upstairs getting dressed when I thought I heard a car in the driveway. By the time I got down, there was no one there—but I found this by the front door. What are they—what are they going to do to me?"

Wendy was holding a battered yearbook. The cover was black with scribbles, and messages had been scrawled in thick black ink throughout the book.

"I—I don't understand. It's a mess, but what's so scary about it?" Nancy asked.

"Look at my class picture!" Wendy gasped. She

flipped through the pages until she came to the right one. Then she pointed a shaking finger at her graduation picture.

It was a beautiful picture—of course. Wendy was smiling serenely at the camera, completely oblivious to what had been scrawled under her name:

Most likely to die!

Chapter

Five

THE YEARBOOK'S NOT all, either!" Wendy said. "This note fell out of the package when I opened it."

Nancy knew what the note would look like even before Wendy held it out. She was right. The letters had been cut from newspaper headlines, and this time the message read, "You'll never steal the scene again."

" 'Steal the scene'?" Nancy repeated as she led Wendy into the Drews' living room. "Do you know what this is about?"

"Of course I don't!" Wendy said. "That is— well, I—no, of course not."

43

But she wasn't meeting Nancy's eyes. "Are you sure?" Nancy asked. "It could be important, you know."

Wendy was still looking away. "Well, there was that musical at the end of our senior year. If you remember, I was in it." She tossed her auburn hair defiantly. "Whoever wrote all over the yearbook kind of—refers to it."

"Can you show me where?" Nancy asked gently.

Reluctantly Wendy held out the book. "On page eighty," she said.

As Nancy leafed through the pages, angry scribbles kept leaping up at her. "Voted the prettiest brat in the class" was written over a shot of Wendy in the homecoming parade. "Pretending she cares," it said next to a shot showing her cheering a winning tackle. "Guess which one is stupider?" asked another scribble next to a shot of Wendy hugging the cheerleaders' mascot—a teddy bear.

Some of the scribbles were more ominous. "You're on your way out. You won't even know what hit you." And, simply, "Get ready."

Then Nancy found the two-page spread of pictures from the senior spring musical—and all at once she did remember what had happened.

It had been the most important play of the year, with a huge cast and a packed auditorium.

As usual, Monica Beckwith had had the lead. Wendy—who'd never been in a high school play before—had had a small part. But no one would have guessed it was small from the way she hammed it up. The audience had been packed with Wendy's friends, and by the second act they were applauding wildly whenever Wendy came onstage.

Someone had been playing tricks on the cast that night—and Monica had borne the brunt of them. A door on the set had crashed to the floor when she'd touched its knob. The tea she was supposed to drink onstage had been salted. Worst of all, someone had cracked a raw egg into the pocket of a coat Monica was supposed to wear onstage. Monica hadn't noticed until she'd reached into the coat pocket. When she'd felt the egg, she'd screamed, burst into tears, and rushed offstage. Her understudy had had to finish the play.

They hadn't ever found out who'd played all those tricks. But Nancy was starting to have a pretty good idea now.

"I was there that night," Nancy said aloud. "It was horrible for Monica."

"Well, you have to admit it was funny," Wendy said, trying not to smile at the memory.

"It might have seemed funny to you, but that was Monica's last school play! Can you imagine how she must have felt?" Nancy protested. "Were you the one who played all those tricks, Wendy?"

Again Wendy refused to meet Nancy's eyes. "Yes, but Patrick thought of some of them. Anyway, that was so long ago," Wendy said slowly. "Why does it matter?"

Patience, Nancy told herself, taking a deep breath. Out loud she said, "Because if you did play them—and someone knows you did—that person might be trying to get even with you now."

"Get even with me!" Now Wendy sounded frightened again. "For a few tricks I played back in high school? They were just jokes! Where's everyone's sense of humor?" She was almost wailing now.

"But, Wendy, it wasn't funny to Monica. Or to anyone else who'd worked so hard on the play."

Now Wendy was off on another tangent. "So you think Monica's the one!" she gasped incredulously. *"She* stole my jewelry and wrecked my room? Are you going to have her arrested?"

"Hang on, hang on!" Nancy said. The last thing she wanted was for Wendy to start jumping to conclusions about the case. "No one's making any arrests or even accusations yet. I'd like to talk to Monica, though. Maybe I should—"

Just then the phone rang. Nancy picked it up.

"Is that you, Nancy?" came a cheerful voice. "This is Patrick Emmons."

"Patrick! How are you feeling? How's your face?"

Patrick laughed. "It's still a little red. It looks as if I'm blushing—all the time. Listen, Wendy told me last night that you're going to be investigating this case. I was wondering if there was any way I could help. I mean, I don't want to get in your way, and I do only have a couple of days before I have to get back to school, but if there's something I could do—"

"That's nice of you," Nancy said sincerely. "The thing is, I don't really have enough to go on to know how you *could* help. But thanks. I'll definitely keep your offer in mind."

"I hope you will. I keep thinking about that doll last night—it gives me the creeps. Do you know how Wendy's doing, by the way? I called her just a minute ago, but I guess she's not home."

"Well, you can find out in person," Nancy said. "She's right here."

"Oh, Patrick, this is all so awful!" Wendy wailed into the receiver. "Rod's not coming back till later this week, and some maniac's out to get me. . . . I *couldn't* tell my parents! They're in Europe! Look, can you have lunch with me? Nancy's on her way over to Monica's now, and I don't have anything to do. . . . Oh. . . . Oh, okay. Well, have fun."

"He's got to do something downtown," she said, disappointed. "Something about lining up a summer job with a law firm for next year. Well, I guess I'll head home."

She looked as if she were hoping Nancy would ask her to come along with her, but Nancy didn't take the hint. She needed to talk to Monica alone.

"Okay," Nancy said. "Talk to you later, Wendy. Is it all right if I take the yearbook with me?"

"Is it all right? Please do." Wendy shuddered. "I never want to see that thing again."

Nancy knew that Monica Beckwith spent most of her time in New York. The River Heights papers loved pieces about local celebrities, and a week never went by without some mention of the local actress making good. But when she was in River Heights, Monica stayed with her parents.

Their house was a couple of miles away from Wendy's. It was a modest two-story cape, nothing at all like Wendy's, and not at all the kind of place where you'd expect a rising star to live. Nancy eased her blue Mustang up to the curb and turned off the ignition.

As she walked up the path to Monica's house, Nancy noticed that the front door was slightly ajar. Then she thought she could hear Monica talking inside, but she sounded strange.

Nancy quickened her pace. Was everything all right in there?

Suddenly Monica's voice turned to a shriek. Nancy raced up the front steps, her heart pounding.

"Now I've got you where I want you!" screamed Monica, laughing insanely.

Bang! went a gun inside the house.

Chapter

Six

NANCY WAS ABOUT to burst through Monica's front door when she froze in her tracks. What if she startled either Monica or whoever had the gun? They might fire at her. She decided to tiptoe.

On the threshold of the front door she heard a whirring noise—and Monica screamed again.

"Now I've got you where I want you!" Again she gave that eerie laugh.

Bang! went the gun.

There was another whirring sound.

"Now I've got you where I want you!" screamed Monica.

Bang!

"Now I've got you where I—"

All of a sudden Nancy knew what the whirring noise was. Trembling with relief, she leaned against the doorframe. "Monica!" she called. "What *are* you doing in there?" Shakily she ran a hand through her hair and stepped into the front hall.

"Oh, hi, Nancy," Monica said sheepishly from the living room, pushing a button near the TV. "I was just watching myself on the VCR. This is a screen test I did for a soap opera. My agent sent it to me a few days ago." She pushed the Play button.

Monica was grinning at Nancy, slightly embarrassed. But on the TV screen, Monica's face was so contorted with fury that Nancy would never have recognized her. She was dressed in black leather and stiletto-heeled black boots, and she was half crouched in the middle of a city street, pointing a gun at the windshield of a gleaming limousine. All around her, passersby were screaming and scrambling to get out of her way. Monica gave that strange laugh and pulled the trigger again. The car's windshield shattered. Monica stepped forward. . . .

And the real Monica stepped forward to press the VCR's Rewind button. The VCR whirred for a few seconds and then clicked off.

"Is that what soaps are like now?" Nancy asked in amazement. "It's been a while since I watched one."

"Oh, no. The producers just wanted to see what kind of range I had. Boy, that screen test put me through everything." Monica giggled. "You should see the part where I had to flirt in a Southern accent. And the part where I had to ride a horse—but anyway, have a seat! I'm sure you didn't come here to watch my screen test."

"Well, you're right," said Nancy. "I've been talking to Wendy this morning."

"Oh, yes?" Monica's face showed nothing but polite interest. "You know, let's go up to my room instead. It's more comfortable up there."

The living room seemed perfectly comfortable, but Nancy followed Monica upstairs anyway.

"Wow!" she said when she saw Monica's bedroom. "I never realized you were so photogenic!"

The walls were entirely covered with pictures of Monica—not an inch of wallpaper showed anywhere, and pictures were stuck in the windows and mirror as well: Monica smiling for a publicity shot; Monica looking wistful in a torn-out page from a magazine interview; Monica glowering at a gorgeous actor who looked vaguely familiar to Nancy.

"That's Gordon Ray," Monica said when she noticed where Nancy was looking. "We did a dinner-theater thing just outside New York. Not quite Broadway, but still— Anyway, there I go again. Sorry! You said you'd been talking to Wendy?"

"Yes—and I've been wondering about a few things." Nancy sat down in a small flowered armchair while Monica perched on the edge of her bed. "First of all, do you have your old yearbook around?"

Before coming to Monica's, Nancy had tucked the one from Wendy in her big shoulder bag so it wouldn't show.

"My yearbook!" Monica said in a startled voice. "Why do you want to know?"

"It may be important to the case." Was Monica stalling?

"Well, as a matter of fact, I—I don't have it here. I had my parents send all that stuff to New York when I got my apartment there."

"So this one's not yours?" Nancy pulled the defaced yearbook from her shoulder bag and watched Monica's face closely to see what her reaction would be.

But Monica's reaction was exactly what Nancy's would have been if anyone had shown her the same book. "No!" she said blankly. "Of course that's not mine. I didn't let people write on the cover. What's going on, Nancy? Look around—you can see for yourself that I don't

53

have any old school stuff here. I would never have
let my yearbook get so messed up, anyway."

"Well, this one was messed up on purpose,"
Nancy said. "Someone sent it to Wendy this
morning. All that writing on it was meant for
her—and *this* is why I wondered if you might
have been the one who owned it." She opened the
yearbook, flipped to the pictures of the class
musical, and held the book out to Monica.

Monica silently studied the pictures and their
message to Wendy. Then she began leafing
through the yearbook page by page. When she
came to the "Most likely to die" page, she
flinched—but she still didn't say a word.

Finally she slammed the book shut. "I can see
why you'd suspect me," she said bitterly and
sarcastically. "I'm *just* the kind of person who'd
do something like this. You know actors—
they're so touchy and temperamental. And I had
such a good excuse, too! Is that what you
thought?"

"I don't really have any opinions yet," said
Nancy mildly. "But I'm sure you can see why I
came here."

"Oh, sure." Monica jumped to her feet and
began pacing back and forth. "Well, one thing's
certainly true. I can't stand Wendy Harriman.
And it's not only because of that musical." She
turned around and glared at Nancy. "Did she
mention Rod to you?"

"The guy she's going with?"

Monica nodded. "That's the one. The guy *I* used to go with." Suddenly her voice broke, and defiantly she brushed away a tear with the back of her hand.

"I met Rod in a summer stock theater near here last year," she continued, sinking down into an armchair. "We really— I know love at first sight sounds silly—but that's just what happened to us. It was all so perfect until I moved to New York. I had introduced him to Wendy at a party, and she just latched onto him when I left. Well, you can imagine the rest. With a girlfriend who was out of town all the time—and Miss Cheerleader coming on to him here at home—next thing I knew, he'd dumped me and was going with Wendy."

Monica blew her nose. "At least he didn't come to the party," she said. "He had a show to do out of town. I read about it in the paper. I wouldn't have gone if he'd been there. So now you can see why I can't stand Wendy," she added. "There's no way I can pretend to like her—even if that makes you think I'm totally guilty."

"Monica, I don't have any clear suspects at this point," Nancy said. "I'm glad you told me all this, though." Better to hear it from you than from somebody else, she thought. "But there's one thing I don't understand—why did you go to the party last night if you hate Wendy so much?"

Monica sighed. "I didn't really want to. But I thought I would feel like a coward if I stayed home. And anyway, I wanted to see everybody else."

"Well, that makes sense," said Nancy. "Look, thanks for talking to me. Will you be around later if I need to ask you anything more?"

"Oh, yes. I'm not going back to New York until next week."

"Good. I'll be in touch, then."

"Uh, Nancy? I wonder if you could do one of your suspects a favor," Monica said. "My car's in the shop, and I've got to go downtown. Is there any chance you could drop me there?"

"No problem," said Nancy. It did seem a little strange to be going out of her way for a possible suspect, but she found it hard to believe Monica could be guilty.

On the other hand, Nancy reminded herself, Monica was an actress—and a good one. She could make herself into almost *any* kind of person. . . .

They were starting downstairs when the phone rang. "I have to get that!" Monica said, dashing into the kitchen to pick it up.

"Hello?" she said eagerly.

Her face fell. "Oh, hi, Wendy," she said coldly. "Yes, she's here. Just a minute." She turned without another word and handed the phone to Nancy.

"Nancy?" Wendy's voice was wobbling. "I—sorry to bother you, but you've got to come over here. I'm in River Heights. Please hurry!"

"I'll be right over," Nancy assured her. She hung up and turned to Monica. "I've got to go to Wendy's before I do anything else. I'll still be glad to take you downtown, though. Do you want me to come back and pick you up?"

"No, no. That'd be too much trouble for you. I'll just come along. It won't kill me to see Wendy. I hope."

"Can you believe this? They took everything! Except for the books, I mean—and who'd bother with those?"

Nancy and Monica had just arrived to find Wendy standing wild-eyed in the family room. Like the rest of the house, the room looked designer-perfect—except for the big, empty gaps in the bookcase where the CD player, tuner, stereo, TV, and VCR had been.

"It must have happened when I was over at your house," Wendy continued. Shivering, she glanced nervously out the window. "It gives me the creeps to think that someone was just hanging around waiting for me to leave! What should I do, Nancy?"

"Well, let's take first things first. Have you called the police?"

"No!"

"I know some of the River Heights police," Nancy said confidently. "We've worked together a few times. I know they'll be helpful—and you don't have a chance of recovering that stuff without them. Let me just give them a ring myself."

In a second she turned around and gave Wendy a reassuring smile. "They're on their way."

When the two officers arrived, Nancy was relieved—she knew both of them. She and Wendy were explaining what had happened when Monica—who had been staring out the window until then—tapped her on the shoulder.

Monica hadn't said a word since they'd gotten to Wendy's. Now she looked worried.

"I hate to cause trouble, but I just remembered that I left some things at home that I'm going to need downtown. But I can see that you should probably stick around here. If you could just drop me off at home, I can call a cab to pick me up."

"Oh, you won't need to do that," said Nancy. "There's nothing more I can do here anyway." She turned to Wendy, who was trying to remember what model the VCR had been. "Wendy, I've got to go," she said. "You're in good hands, I promise. I'll give you a call as soon as I can." But Wendy kept Nancy there with questions. It was twenty more minutes before they left.

"That's strange," Nancy said to Monica as

they were pulling up to her house. "I could have sworn you locked the front door when we left."

Monica's front door was half open and swinging gently on its hinges.

"I *did* lock it," said Monica. "I heard it click. Maybe my mother's home. But I don't see her car anywhere. I wonder if the wind—"

She was out of the car and racing up the walk before Nancy could get out.

Nancy followed slowly. She had a nagging feeling she knew what they were going to find.

And she was right. A grim-faced Monica met her at the door.

"Someone's been here, too!" she gasped. "And whoever it is may still be in the house!"

Chapter

Seven

Monica's teeth were chattering. "The living room is wrecked," she whispered. "And I heard—I think I heard—someone running upstairs when I came in."

Then she gasped. "My screen-test video! I left it up in my room!" And before Nancy could stop her, she had turned and rushed into the house again.

"Monica! Come back! The burglar may be in your room!" Nancy called frantically. But all she could hear were Monica's feet thudding up the stairs.

There was nothing Nancy could do but follow her. If the burglar was still in the house, both girls were in terrible danger—but it was too late to hold back now.

Nancy threw a glance at the living room as she rushed by. It looked as though it had been torn apart, and both the TV and VCR were gone. She'd have to check that out later. She dashed up to Monica's room.

One of the windows in the room was open. Nancy rushed across to it and stuck her head out, being careful not to touch the sill in case there were any fingerprints. She could see that there wasn't much of a drop from there, and the thick hemlock bushes below would have broken the fall of anyone who had jumped. Were those footprints in the dirt bed which bordered the bushes? She couldn't tell.

Nancy turned to Monica, who was standing in the middle of the room. "Well, I found the tape," said Monica with a bleak smile.

She was holding an empty VCR cassette. The tape had been yanked from it and draped all over her room. Festoons of it hung from the ceiling light and the curtain rods, and a tangled mass of tape lay snarled on the bed.

That wasn't all. The pictures on Monica's walls had been covered with angry black scribbles. Childishly drawn beards adorned some of the faces, but most of the pictures had messages on them. Ugly messages—and probably the work of the same person who'd defaced that yearbook.

"I know that window was closed when we left," said Monica. "We always keep the windows closed when the air conditioning's on."

"Then this must be how he or she got out."

"Probably a she. Look at this, Nancy." Monica pointed at a piece of paper on her desk.

The cut-out letters were all too familiar: "Don't waste your time. You couldn't act your way into a used-car commercial."

"Nice style, don't you think?" Monica asked dryly.

"Lovely," answered Nancy. "But why do you think it's from a girl?"

"Because Celia Quaid once said those exact words to me back in high school. I'd asked her if she was going to see a play I was in that weekend. I was just making conversation, but I guess she must have thought I sounded conceited or something. So she said that to me right in front of everyone. Then she stood up and walked out of the room. I couldn't have made a better exit myself."

"I can imagine," said Nancy. It looked as though Celia would have to be the next person she interviewed. And it also looked as though Nancy could rule Monica out as a suspect. There was no way Monica could have robbed her own house while she was at Wendy's.

"Look, Nancy, I'm going to forget going downtown after all," Monica said. "I'll cancel my appointment. I think I'd better be here when my mother gets home."

"Good idea," Nancy said. "And you'd also better call the police. We need to report another robbery."

"But Nancy, it's one o'clock!" Bess protested. "Don't you want to eat first?"

Nancy was calling Bess from Monica's house. She wanted to see Celia right away, and now that the police had arrived she felt it would be all right to leave Monica alone.

"No. I really can't think about food until I've seen Celia," she told Bess. "And I'd love it if you could be there to back me up. Could you possibly meet me in, say, forty-five minutes? Thanks, Bess. . . . *No,* you don't need to bring me a sandwich!"

Nancy hung up the phone. Monica was showing the two officers the damage in the living room.

"Monica, if you think you can handle this on your own, I'm going to go," Nancy said. "Does Celia live near here?"

"About twenty minutes away. Good luck," Monica added.

When Nancy arrived at Celia's apartment building, Bess wasn't there. So she decided to park her car and take a walk while she waited the twenty-five minutes.

The late-summer sun felt wonderful, and Nancy suddenly realized she had spent the last five and a half hours—since eight o'clock—either inside talking to Wendy and Monica or in her car on the way to their houses. She checked her watch. There was a little park near there, she knew, and if she walked fast she'd get there and back in plenty of time.

But she hadn't made it all the way to the park when she heard footsteps pounding up behind her. A male voice called out, "Nancy! Wait up!"

It was Don Cameron.

"What an incredible coincidence!" he said. He was beaming with happiness, and his brown eyes were sparkling. "First the party, and now this! Boy, I'm glad I decided not to go back to school early. What are you doing here, anyway?"

"I—I was just going to ask you the same thing," Nancy said. She knew she sounded cold, but she couldn't help it. Talking to Don was pretty low on the list of things she felt like doing right then. But Don hadn't noticed her tone—and he didn't seem to want to answer her question.

"You know, Nancy," he said, "seeing you at

the party yesterday really got me thinking. I thought you were out of my system, but—well, do you think we could try again? I haven't met anyone like you at college. And we had such great times together, didn't we? I can't have imagined the whole thing, can I?"

What is the *matter* with him? Nancy thought despairingly. Anyone else would have gotten the message yesterday! She cleared her throat and tried again.

"Yes, we did have some good times. But, Don, that was a long time ago! I think you're a great guy, but I'm in love with Ned. I just can't see you and me getting back together. I'm sorry."

Now Don looked as though she'd slapped him. "But now that I've been away, I'm more convinced than ever that you're really special!" he pleaded. "There's really no one like you at college."

"Well, Don, I'm sorry about that, too, but there's really nothing I can do," said Nancy. "Maybe it'll take you a little time—"

"Don! Nancy! How's it going?"

Startled, both Nancy and Don turned to see Patrick Emmons's black Corvette pulling up next to them. "Hi, guys!" he said cheerfully. "Hey, this is just like old times, seeing you together!"

"Not exactly," Don muttered.

"Just don't let Nickerson find out you're here,

Don," Patrick said jokingly. "He wouldn't want you stealing his girl in broad daylight—"

Then he suddenly seemed to sense the tension between Don and Nancy, and he looked away. "Uh-oh. Sorry if I'm interrupting anything," he said awkwardly.

"You aren't!" Nancy said a little more emphatically than she had meant to. "I was on my way to Celia's, and"—she checked her watch again— "it looks as though I'm going to be really late. Nice seeing both of you!" She dashed away before either boy could say another word.

Bess was waiting in her car in front of Celia's house. She jumped out when she saw Nancy. "I thought you said this was urgent!" she protested.

Nancy sighed. "It is. Sorry *I'm* late," she said. "I ran into Don Cameron on the way. Getting rid of him took a lot longer than it should have." If she'd succeeded at all, she reminded herself miserably.

Celia lived by herself in a small apartment near the local junior college. The apartment was on the first floor of a small brick building. Her name was printed in tiny letters under the doorbell. Nancy pressed the bell firmly and waited. No answer. She rang the bell again. "I hear someone in there," she whispered, and she rang again. "She knows we're coming. I called her from Monica's."

It took two more tries before they heard someone walking up to the door. Then it opened a crack, and Celia peered out at them.

Again Nancy was amazed at how beautiful Celia had become—and how angry she seemed. "Oh, there you are," Celia said coldly, as though they'd been the ones keeping her waiting. "I was back in my room."

Silently she led the way into the apartment. She plopped herself down in a chair without inviting them to join her. After a moment's hesitation, Nancy sat down, too, and Bess followed suit.

Nancy decided to get to the point right away. Her high-backed wooden chair was too uncomfortable to relax in, and Celia's expression was so sour that she couldn't imagine trying to have a conversation with her.

"A lot of weird things have been happening since Wendy's party last night," Nancy said. "I was wondering if you knew anything about—"

"Kerchoo!" Bess reddened with embarrassment. "Sorry," she said, blowing her nose.

Nancy tried again. "For example, is this your yearb—"

"Kerchoo! Kerchoo!" Nancy and Celia both turned to look at Bess. "I'm really sorry," she said again.

"Someone sent Wendy this yearbook earlier today, and I was wondering if—"

"Kerchoo!" Now Bess was beet red. "I don't

67

know what's going on," she said. "I must be allergic to something. I can smell paint. Are you painting?"

"Yes," Celia responded.

"The only thing that gets me started this way is oil-base paint, and—"

"I'm using oil-base in my room," Celia interrupted.

"Oh, no," Bess said. "Then we have a little bit of a problem. This sneezing's not going to let up. Believe me, I *know* it's not." She blew her nose and cast an apologetic look at Nancy. "I could go wait in the car or something—"

"Why don't we all go outside?" suggested Nancy. "I started to take a walk earlier, and I didn't get to finish it. Celia, would that be okay?"

Celia shrugged. "I guess there's no reason why not," she said.

This is a total dead end, Nancy thought wearily, thirty minutes later. Not that I expected Celia to confess—but she's not going to tell us *anything!*

Nancy had described the robberies at Wendy's and Monica's, and Celia hadn't responded at all. She had shown Celia the yearbook as they had been walking along, and all Celia had done was cackle with laughter and say that Wendy had it coming to her. Celia utterly refused to talk about anything that had happened in high school.

Suddenly Nancy decided to try a different strategy. "You know, I'm not sure if you realize that you're my prime suspect," Nancy said. "Do you *want* me to think you're guilty? Because you're doing a pretty good imitation of someone who does."

Celia stopped short in the middle of the sidewalk. "And I'm not sure if *you* realize that all *I* want to do is forget about high school. Why should I care what's happened to Wendy, or Monica, for that matter? And why would I do something that would mean I'd have to remember those days again?"

"So why'd you go to the party?" Bess blurted.

"Because I wanted to show all of you what I'd done! To show you that I *could* do it! None of you can possibly imagine what it was like back then," Celia continued. "You were all popular. No one made fun of you, or if they did"—Bess had started to protest—"it was because they liked you. Do you know how it felt to be the class joke? To know that people were making fun of me because they *didn't* like me?

"I was finally able to lose all that weight when I moved out of my parents' house and started going to college. That was the first time I wasn't around anyone who had any kind of, well, former impression of me.

"I know I seem a little unpleasant, but I can't stand being around people who remind me of high school. That doesn't mean I'm guilty. I'm not, Nancy—really. There wouldn't be any point in my trying to get revenge now. The girl I used to be—the one who *deserves* revenge for the way people treated her—is gone. And I hope she'll never come back."

Nancy had to admit it all sounded plausible. But she didn't want to let Celia go before she had more information.

"I understand what you're saying, but I think I've still got to ask you some more questions—even if you don't want to answer them," she said. "Whether or not you want to be involved, you *are*. If you're telling the truth—and someone is framing you—then the only way to separate yourself from all this high school stuff is to talk to me."

Celia sighed. "Okay. But I did promise myself I'd finish painting my room by suppertime. Can we go back to my apartment and keep talking in there? I know Bess won't be able to—"

"I can go home," Bess broke in. "I'll meet you later, Nan. I'll pick up George and check out the beach house. Okay?"

Nancy thought it was a great idea. She had planned to go there herself but hadn't had the time.

"Okay, Celia. It'll be fine to go back to your house. Maybe there's even something I can help you with."

"Actually, I don't need any help," Celia said when they'd reached her room. "Doing the molding is a one-person job. You can just ask me your questions, and I'll keep painting." She picked up her brush and can of shell-pink paint and started climbing up the ladder that was standing on a dropcloth at one side of the room.

As she stepped on the top rung her foot crashed right through, and she lost her balance. Desperately she grabbed for the ladder, paint flying from the can and showering the room before the quart container banged to the floor.

"No!" Celia gasped as she tried to cling by her fingertips to the top platform. The ladder started to sway back and forth as she struggled to hook her feet onto a step. Finally, her weight pulled the ladder forward, and she landed on the floor with a sickening thud. The ladder clattered down on top of her.

For a second the sound of the crash echoed through the little room. Then there was a terrible silence.

Chapter

Eight

D<small>ON'T MOVE, CELIA</small>!" Nancy said quickly, springing forward to lift the heavy ladder off the still body. She pulled it to one side, then knelt down next to the other girl. "Are you all right?" she asked.

Celia shook her head and tried to push herself up on her hands, but she collapsed immediately. "I can't get up," she moaned. "My arm won't move. I felt something snap when I fell."

"It does look broken to me," Nancy said. The arm was bent backward at a frightening angle. And above Celia's eye a huge, purple, egglike bruise was puffing up. The ladder must have hit her on her head, Nancy realized. "Don't try to move," Nancy said quickly. "I'm going to call an ambulance right now."

"There's a phone in the next room. . . . " Celia said, her voice trailing off.

The call took only a few minutes. When Nancy came back, Celia was straining to look around. "Did much of the paint spill?" she asked.

Nancy smiled. "Nope. Just all of it!"

"I can't believe I was so clumsy," Celia gasped. "I never—"

"You weren't clumsy." Nancy's voice had suddenly turned hard. She'd just noticed the top rung of the ladder.

It had been sawed clear through. And there was a tiny note taped to the top platform. No one climbing the ladder would have been able to see it. It was clearly meant to be visible only to someone at the top of the ladder.

"You see," the note jeered, "you're the same fat loser you always were."

"What's that?" Celia asked.

Nancy couldn't bring herself to read the note aloud. She just showed it to Celia—and watched as a different kind of pain spread across the injured girl's face.

"Do you have any idea who might have done this?" Nancy asked.

There were tears in Celia's eyes. "It can only be from Judd Reese," she said. "He always used to call me Fat Loser back in school. Then he shortened it to F.L. I guess I was wrong. I'll never be able to get away from high school. Will you catch him, Nancy?" she asked in a tiny voice.

The ambulance was just pulling up outside. "You bet I will," said Nancy as she got up to answer the door. "Whoever it was. Now we're going to help you get to the hospital. I'll call your parents, and they can be there by the time you arrive. Now you just think about getting better."

Bess would have been relieved. It was five o'clock, and Nancy was finally back at home getting some lunch.

She'd just called the hospital and talked to Celia, who was doing fine. Her parents were with her. Her arm was broken and had been set, and she was going to spend the night in the hospital just to make sure her head was okay. There was no sign of a concussion, though, and no other injuries except bruises.

That was a relief, anyway. But Nancy had also talked to the police—and their news was less good. They had no leads on the two new robberies that had taken place earlier that day. No fingerprints had been left anywhere. And of course there was no trace of the stuff that had been stolen from any of the houses.

"I can hardly believe this is the work of a kid, Nancy," one of the officers said to her. "If it weren't for those notes, I'd say we were dealing with a pro."

Was Judd a pro? Nancy would find out the next day. She called Bess and found out she and George had discovered no clues at the beach house.

Nancy decided to forget about the case for that night. She and Ned had plans to see a movie. He'd be coming by in an hour to pick her up, and she still had shell-pink paint to remove from her hair and skin. For the next couple of hours, the only thing she wanted to think about was being with Ned.

"You're sure you'll be okay with Judd?" Ned asked as they walked home after the movie. "I mean, if he does turn out to be guilty?"

"Well, I don't expect to be alone," Nancy said. "He works in a big garage over on Church Street. I called him and made plans to see him at ten in the morning. But it's sweet of you to be worried." She stopped and stood on tiptoe to kiss him.

"Oh, I'm not really worried, Nan," Ned said. "I just wish there was something I could do to help you with the case. *Is* there something?"

Nancy smiled. "Not so far," she said, "but there is one thing you could do for me right now."

"Yes?" Ned asked, raising one eyebrow like a villain in an old-time movie.

"Well, *after* you kiss me, could we stop for ice cream somewhere? I don't want to sound like Bess, but I'm *starving*. I don't think I can walk another step if I don't get some ice cream right away."

As Nancy eased her car into a parking place across from the Church Street Garage the next morning, she wondered how Judd could possibly stand to work where he did. Right next door to the garage was a record store with the loudest music she'd ever heard pouring out of two speakers in front of the building.

By the time she had parked her car and started across the street, Nancy's ears were throbbing. And when Judd came striding out to meet her, he had to yell to be heard above the music.

"Come on into my office," he shouted. "I'm guessing that whatever you have to talk to me about, you don't want to do it out here in the open."

Nancy smiled in spite of herself. "Good guess," she shouted back. "I don't think you could hear me, anyway."

Luckily, the noise eased up once they were inside the garage. On the way back to Judd's office Nancy couldn't help noticing a black Corvette on a hydraulic lift. "That's not Patrick Emmons's, is it?" she asked.

"Uh-huh," Judd tossed back over his shoulder. "I heard the brakes are shot."

Nancy was surprised. Wasn't Patrick's car brand-new? But Judd had already disappeared into the office ahead of her, and she had to hurry to catch up with him.

Before he sat down behind the desk, he scooped a pile of old magazines off the only other chair in the office. "Have a seat," he said. "Sorry about the background noise. They keep that music on all day. It really drives me crazy."

"I can see why." Nancy wasn't quite sure how to begin. "You've been working here since high school?" she asked casually.

"That's right. My uncle owns the place, and he pretty much lets me run it. He says that if I work hard enough he'll make me a partner next year." Judd's offhanded tone couldn't quite hide the pride in his eyes. "I thought when I first started that it'd be easy, but I'm sure working harder than I ever did in school. Except that I'm going to school now, too."

"You are?" Nancy asked, then hoped she hadn't sounded too surprised.

"Yup. I'm taking some college courses at night. I don't know if I'll get my degree. But I want options. I don't know if I want to spend my whole life in a garage."

"Well, that sounds great," Nancy said lamely. She wasn't sure how to go on from here—until Judd made it easy for her.

"You here to talk about what happened at Wendy's the other night?" he asked.

"That's right—and a couple of other things."

Judd didn't react as Nancy described everything that had happened the day before. He just leaned back in his chair, looking bored. But when she got to the part about the sawed-through ladder rung at Celia's, he straightened up abruptly.

"That's a shame," he said unexpectedly. "After everything she's done to turn her life around. But who could have anything against *Celia?*"

"Well—uh—I've got to admit I was wondering if it might be you, Judd." She pulled the note to Celia out of her purse and showed it to him.

Judd read the note, and read it again. When he passed it back to her, his eyes were wary. "So?" he said defensively. "What does this have to do with me?"

Nancy wasn't enjoying this. She'd never really known Judd in high school, and she'd only seen him around a couple of times since graduation. The Judd she was talking to now seemed totally different from the image she had formed of him in high school. He seemed far too likable to be guilty. But don't start rooting for him! she told herself. He's your strongest suspect now!

"So Celia told me you used to call her Fat Loser in high school. Is that true?"

Judd rubbed the back of his neck and looked away, dropping his eyes. "Yeah. It is. But people do lots of stupid things in high school. And I sure wasn't the only person who made fun of Celia back then—even though I may be the only person who's sorry about it now."

"Did anyone else call her that?"

"I don't know," Judd answered back a little snappishly.

"Judd, I'm sorry," Nancy said. "But do you have any proof of where you were yesterday afternoon? I'm just trying to get at the truth—"

"Sure you are." Judd was on his feet now, and leaning into her across the desk. "The real truth is that people like me are always in trouble—no matter what the facts are. Isn't that right?"

"No. If you haven't done anything wrong, then you don't have anything to worry about!"

"Of course I do. I have to worry about being branded a punk for the rest of my life just because I didn't make Eagle Scout. Why would I do a thing like that to Celia? Or Monica? Or Wendy—even though she might deserve it?"

"What do you mean, she might deserve it?"

"Okay, I shouldn't have said that. But when I was a freshman she found out I had a crush on her, and she never let me forget it. She used to call me and talk to me for a minute or two, then hang up. Once she even made a date with me. She never showed. It was like she wanted to keep reminding me that I wasn't good enough for her—but at the same time she kept leading me on."

Judd shook his head. "That showed me what some girls are like. But do you think I'd *rob* her because of something that happened freshman year? If *I've* changed, I've got to give her credit for changing, too—if she has."

"I'm sorry" was all Nancy said. "Just tell me what you were doing yesterday afternoon, and I'll go."

"I don't have to tell you anything," Judd said quietly. "You've got a good imagination. I'm sure you'll make something up. Now I'm getting out of here *before* I lose my temper."

"Just a gentle hour alone with you—" trilled the speakers next door. They had just been jammed up to full volume.

Judd slammed his fist into the desk. "That music!" he yelled. "Someday I'm going to kill that guy! Okay, I'm leaving. And when I come back, I don't want to see you here."

"Judd!" But he was gone.

Nancy drew a shaky breath. She hadn't done anything wrong—but she still felt uneasy and tense.

What was a good detective supposed to do at a time like this? She could hardly think straight.

Then the answer came to her as if someone had dictated it. "A good detective would use this chance to search Judd's office."

But what was there to search for in a garage office? The row of phone books above the desk? The dusty calendar on the wall? The wastebasket?

The wastebasket. When Nancy glanced down at it, she could hardly believe she hadn't noticed it before.

Judd's wastebasket was stuffed with old newspapers. And all of their headlines had been cut out!

Chapter

Nine

WAS JUDD THE culprit after all? Nancy assumed she had solved the case already and wondered why she felt totally unsatisfied.

It's just that it's so hard to believe! she told herself. True, everything pointed to Judd now. He'd made it clear to Nancy that he had a grudge against Wendy. He'd been the person Celia had first suspected. And now to find all those newspapers with the words cut out.

It had to be Judd, Nancy thought, trying to convince herself. That meant that every impression he had just given Nancy had been wrong.

Slowly Nancy reached into the wastebasket to pick up the cut-up newspapers. At that exact moment Judd walked back in.

"Come into the office and have a seat, sir. I'll just get those forms for you to sign," he was saying politely to someone behind him. Then he caught sight of Nancy. "Oh, excuse me a minute," he said to his customer. "I'll be right with you."

He stepped toward Nancy so menacingly that she dropped the papers and backed away. When he spoke, his voice was cool—too cool.

"I thought I'd asked you to do something pretty simple, Nancy," he said. "Why are you still here?"

Nancy's heart was pounding. She knew she had nothing to be afraid of, but Judd looked so blazingly angry that she felt frightened—and as guilty as if she'd been the one caught stealing. "I—I forgot something," she stammered.

"Have you remembered it now?"

Nancy nodded.

"Okay. Then get out."

Nancy grabbed her shoulder bag and left. It wasn't until she was safely back in her car across the street that she realized she hadn't brought any of the newspapers with her. And they were her only evidence!

Nancy leaned back in her seat and let out a

long, frustrated sigh. "Boy, Drew," she muttered aloud. "You really blew it."

Should she go back and get the papers? Nancy almost laughed at the idea. She could just imagine walking back into Judd's office—in front of his customer—and trying to take the papers out of his wastebasket.

No, the papers would just have to stay there—if they were still there at all. Nancy was sure Judd had noticed what she was doing. He'd probably already gotten rid of them.

Sighing again, Nancy put the key into the ignition. As she did so she glanced over at the garage one last time. She couldn't see into Judd's office; all she could see was Patrick's gleaming black Corvette up on the lift.

Patrick's Corvette . . . Suddenly Nancy's thoughts took a new direction. If Judd *was* guilty of all these other attacks, wasn't it possible Patrick was in danger, too? All the kids who had been attacked had been successful in some way. If Judd resented people who were more successful than he was, who better to resent than Patrick?

And if Patrick was next on Judd's hit list, wouldn't sabotaging Patrick's car be a great way to get him?

Nancy decided she had to follow up on her hunch. She drove to a pay phone around the corner and called Patrick at home.

Five rings. Six. Answer, answer, Nancy thought impatiently. I want *something* to go right today. At last Patrick picked up, on the eighth ring.

"Nancy, hi!" he said enthusiastically after hearing her voice. "I was working out in the yard. How are things going?"

"Fine, I guess. But let me ask you one question before I forget. What's the matter with your car?" Nancy tried to sound casual.

"Oh, nothing, really," said Patrick. "It's only a couple of months old, you know! It just needs its thousand-mile check. Is that why you called?" he added with a laugh.

"No. But it tells me I was right to call," Nancy said. "Can you meet me at Pete's Place in half an hour? I need to talk to you right away."

Pete's Place was a little coffee shop about ten minutes from the high school. It was famous for its onion rings, which were pretty much the only good thing on the menu. Nancy hadn't been there since high school—and the minute she stepped in the door, she could remember why. The place smelled as though everything in it had been dipped in a frying vat.

Patrick was already waiting in a booth when Nancy got there. "The menu hasn't changed much," he said. "A double order of rings and two Cokes?" he asked Nancy, and after she nodded yes he told the waitress. "At least Pete's makes me realize college food isn't so bad. That's the one thing I'm not looking forward to about going back—that and the long drive. I still haven't found anyone to share the trip with me."

"Actually," Nancy said, "it's your car I wanted to talk to you about. Or not your car, exactly, but Judd Reese."

"What do you mean?" Patrick asked. "I've heard he does a great job. A million people have recommended that garage—"

"No, no, it's not the garage," Nancy interrupted. "It's just that I was talking to Judd earlier today, and he told me the brakes on your car were shot. Did he mention that to you?"

"No." Patrick looked amazed. "How could there be any problem with them? The car's brand-new."

"Patrick, I don't want to worry you, but I think Judd may be the guy who's behind all these robberies."

"All *what* robberies? Has something else happened since the party?"

"Has something else happened! Oh, that's right—you don't know. Sorry. Let me start from the beginning."

Just then the waitress set down two huge platters of golden brown onion rings in front of them. "These will keep us going for a while, anyway," Patrick said as he picked up the salt shaker. "Tell me everything."

So Nancy told him everything, and by the time she had reached the part about Celia, Patrick was looking a little sick.

"This is too much," he said. "Whoever's behind this is one weird guy. That's all I can say. But you can't really believe it's Judd, Nancy! He's not smart enough to pull something like this."

"Well, I might have agreed with you until I talked to him this morning." Quickly Nancy described the scene in Judd's office. "I may be worrying for nothing," she finished, "but I think you're next on his list, Patrick. Why else would he have made up that story about your car? This is the perfect chance for him to sabotage it."

"No." Patrick spoke very firmly. "That's just not possible. I know Judd's a little different from us, but he's not a bad guy. Maybe he thought you were talking about a different car—"

"No, yours was the only one up on the lift—"

"Then there must be some other mistake."

"What about the newspapers?" Nancy persisted.

"Don't know. It sounds as though you didn't get a chance to see them up close." Nancy blushed, remembering how jittery she'd been in Judd's office. "I don't want to sound as though

I'm criticizing you, Nancy, but I just don't think Judd's up to doing something like this."

"You sound as though you have someone else in mind—someone definite," Nancy said.

"Well, I—well, no. Not really, I mean."

"Patrick, what's the matter? Do you know something I don't?" Nancy asked.

"I—" Patrick looked away. "Well, I do have kind of an idea—but it wouldn't really be fair to mention it. Not without more to go on. Besides, I don't want to make things awkward for you."

"Awkward?" Nancy repeated. "Patrick, please. If you think you know something I've missed, just tell me."

"Well," Patrick said after a pause, "remember, I'm not at all sure about this—but I think you might want to check out Don Cameron."

"Don Cameron!" Nancy was so startled she almost choked on an onion ring.

Patrick looked embarrassed. "I know that it's hard for you to hear, when you used to be so close to him—"

"No, no," Nancy interrupted. "That's not a problem. It's just that—I can hardly believe Don's the type to do something like this."

But as she spoke, she suddenly remembered how odd Don had been acting the day before. Was it really possible that he'd turned into a different person since high school?

Patrick was looking steadily at her. "I know it's

hard to believe," he said. "It was hard for me, too. Don was a pretty good friend of mine in school, you know. But look at the facts, Nancy. He's been on the scene at some pretty strange times, hasn't he? You said he was nearby when you discovered the hornets in Ned's car. And I saw him talking to you yesterday—wasn't that just before you found out that Monica's house had been robbed? I wish that it didn't all point to him, but I can't figure things out any other way."

"It still seems impossible," Nancy said slowly. But even as she spoke the words she was realizing that Patrick might be right. She pushed away her plate and leaned her cheek on her hand. "But if it's true—"

"It's got to be true, Nancy." Patrick's voice was suddenly tense. "Look behind you."

Nancy whirled around, but all she saw was a bored-looking waitress cleaning the booth behind them.

"No. Outside. Beside your car."

Nancy followed his gaze—and gasped. Don was standing right next to her Mustang. And as she watched, he opened the door and climbed inside!

Chapter
Ten

F OR A SECOND Nancy sat absolutely still.

I can't go out, she thought. I just don't want to confront him. It'll be so embarrassing!

It had been hard enough trying to make Don see that she wasn't interested in him. But treating him like a suspect now? That was impossibly mean—and impossibly awkward.

Still, she'd have to do it sometime. She might as well get it over with now. Slowly Nancy stood up.

"Want me to come with you in case he tries anything?" Patrick asked quietly.

"No. No thanks, I mean. He won't try anything. I have to clear this up myself. Oh, the check—"

"No, no. I'll take care of the tab," Patrick said.

"Thanks." Nancy just managed a smile, then headed out the door.

She'd parked the Mustang across the street. Now the door on the driver's side was open, and Don was sitting inside scribbling something on a piece of paper.

Another note! At first Nancy's heart leaped, but then she reminded herself that *that* didn't prove anything. The other notes weren't handwritten.

In the few seconds it took to walk out of the restaurant's door, Nancy had decided to act as unsuspecting as possible. "Hi, Don!" she called out in a cheerful voice. "What can I do for you?"

"Nancy! Uh, hi! I—"

Hastily Don scrambled out of her car. "I—I didn't expect you back so soon." Nervously he pushed his hair out of his eyes. "I mean— I don't mean it that way. That is—I was just writing you a note. Here it is." He held the piece of paper out to her without appearing to notice that he'd already crumpled it up. Then he pulled his hand back and stuffed the note into the front pocket of his jeans. "On second thought, let me just tell you what it says. You wouldn't be able to read my writing."

Nancy was longing to tell him to relax, but she kept quiet. Out of the corner of her eye she could see Patrick walking out of the restaurant. He stopped for a second, but Don didn't notice him, and Patrick walked slowly away.

"Look, I know I made a fool of myself yesterday," Don said rapidly. "I kept waking up in the night and remembering how stupid I must have sounded."

"You didn't sound stupid, Don," Nancy said. "Just a little—well, a little like someone who didn't believe what he was hearing."

"I believed it. Believe me, I believed it," Don answered glumly. "But, Nancy, I'm going to have to make a fool of myself again. I can't help it. Would you please at least consider going out with me just one more time? Just to—well, just so we could talk? I promise I'll never ask again."

Oh, no, Nancy thought. What should I do?

If she agreed to go out with Don, she risked going out on a date with a guy who might be crazy. A guy who might have spent the last few days on a weird spree of revenge and who might think he had great reasons for wanting revenge on Nancy, too.

On the other hand, a date with Don might be the perfect way to find out whether he was guilty or not. It might be the only way, in fact.

"I guess it wasn't such a great idea," she heard Don say. His face was getting redder and redder, and Nancy realized she'd been standing silent for a long time. She hoped her indecision hadn't been too obvious, because she'd made up her mind what her answer should be.

"I'd be happy to spend some time with you," she said. But not for the reason you think, she added to herself. "How about tonight?"

"You mean you'd really like to? Well, where shall we go?" Don asked. "There's a great restaurant at the top of the Hargreave Building. Very private. They seat you in these little curtained banquettes—"

No way! Nancy thought. A nice private evening with Don was the last thing she wanted. She needed a place where they could talk easily *and* where Nancy could be sure she was safe.

"I know!" Nancy said. "Remember how much we used to love Rosedale Park?" Rosedale was an amusement park about half an hour out of River Heights. Nancy had been there with Don when they'd first started dating. "Why don't we go there?"

Don looked startled. "Rosedale! What do you mean, we used to love it? We only went there once."

"But I've never forgotten what fun it was," Nancy said quickly. "Really, Don, I can't think of a place I'd like better."

"Well, if you're sure—" Don said in a disappointed voice.

"Oh, I think it sounds perfect," Nancy answered. "And, look, why don't I drive?" If Don *was* guilty, she wanted to be the one in the driver's seat.

"But there's no reason— Oh, well, I might as well not push my luck," said Don. "But don't bother picking me up. My little brother's going to a night soccer game, and he can drop me off at your place. What time's good for you?"

"I'll be ready at seven-thirty," said Nancy. Ready to see exactly what you're up to, she added to herself.

Seven-fifteen. Nancy was in her room studying herself in the mirror and biting her lip.

For once she was glad her father and Hannah were out of town. It would have been hard to explain why she was seeing Don again.

She'd been trying to get in touch with Ned all afternoon to explain what she was doing. But there had been no answer. Nancy hated to leave without filling Ned in, but it didn't look as though she had a choice.

Well, she'd have to worry about that later. Now she was wondering what she should wear. She didn't want to look as if she'd dressed up for Don, but she didn't want to offend him by looking like a slob, either. She'd finally settled on a denim miniskirt and an oversize lilac T-shirt.

But now she decided that maybe she'd better

change into something less sporty. Just as Nancy was walking toward her closet, though, the doorbell rang. She ran down to answer it.

"Don, you're ten minutes early—" she started to say as she opened the door. But it wasn't Don.

It was Ned.

"I guess you weren't expecting me," he said dryly.

"Ned! Oh, no!" Nancy blurted out before she could stop herself. "No, I wasn't expecting you," she said more calmly. "Something's come up—something connected with the case. I've got to go out with—"

The doorbell rang again. "Nancy?" Don called.

Ned was staring at Nancy. "You're going out with Don?" he asked.

"Yes, but—"

"Well, that's just great." Ned was pale with anger. Nancy longed to tell him that this was nothing more than a chance to investigate a potential suspect, but it was too late. No matter how upset Ned was, he'd have to wait for the explanation.

"Nancy? Are you there?" Don called.

Ned yanked the front door open. "Yes, she's here," he said grimly. "Have fun, you two." He strode back to his car. With a screech of tires, he backed out of the driveway and roared up the street.

Don was staring at Nancy. "I, uh—I guess I came at a bad time," he said.

"Forget it," Nancy said bleakly. "Let's go."

"Timmy! You get over here right now!" squalled a woman.

"Oops! Sorry, miss," said Timmy, who had just crashed into Nancy while running back to his mom.

"That's okay," Nancy said, watching him dash off. She looked down and sighed. When Timmy had bumped into her, he had smashed his ice-cream cone into her knee.

As a setting for investigating Don, Rosedale Park wasn't working out. It was true that there was no danger of Nancy's being stuck alone with him. But it was equally true that it was almost impossible to talk to him at all—at least not on the rides they'd already taken. Only the Ferris wheel had offered a chance for conversation. But the minute they'd gotten aloft, the kids in the car above theirs had started screaming, so Nancy and Don couldn't hear each other.

Don was starting to look more and more glum. Nancy couldn't help feeling a little remorse for having led him on. He still thought they were on a date, and he probably thought it was his fault they weren't having any fun.

It was time to put an end to all this. But just as

Nancy was about to suggest that they go home, Don suddenly said, "Look! I remember the last time we rode on *that.* Let's give it another try. At least it'll be quiet in there."

He was pointing to the Tunnel of Love, whose sign blared, "Take a fun-filled trip into the heart of romance!" A line of expectant-looking couples was just beginning to take seats in the boat. "Let's get on before the boat fills up!" Don said.

It wasn't the perfect setting for the questions Nancy wanted to ask Don, but at least the tunnel wouldn't be filled with shrieking kids. "Okay. Let's go."

Before they climbed into the boat, Nancy looked down at the water in the tunnel—and shuddered. It was green and slimy, and cigarette butts were floating in it. Boy, I'll go to any length to solve a case, she thought to herself.

In silence she and Don climbed into the shabby boat, and in silence they rode it into the dark tunnel. "Eric, I'm scared!" the girl in front of them said as she snuggled into her boyfriend's arms.

Uh-oh, Nancy thought. She could tell by the meaningful way Don cleared his throat that he was about to get serious.

She was right. "Uh, Nancy, I've been wanting to say this all evening—" Don began.

Nancy couldn't stand to let him get any further. She started talking before he could say another word.

"Don, there's something I've been wanting to say all evening, too. I don't know if you've heard, but Wendy and Monica were both robbed the day after the party. It looks as though the burglar was the same person who broke into Wendy's beach house. Also Celia's house was booby-trapped. I think I've narrowed down my list of suspects to just a couple of people, and I was wondering if I could ask you a few questions."

"What?"

The boat lurched as he violently jerked around to face her.

"Hey, cut it out!" the girl in front of them protested.

Don didn't seem to notice. "What's going on here?" he hissed. "Is this all a setup? Is that the kind of person you think I am? Well, let me tell you something—"

In the dim light his face looked ghastly—white and almost wraithlike. Alarmed, Nancy just stared back at him.

He can't do anything, she thought. There are people all around us—

Then Don abruptly moved toward her. Suddenly Nancy was sure he was going to attack.

"I'll *show* you what kind of person I am!" Don growled.

Nancy jumped to her feet. "Get away from me!" she cried.

"No, wait! Nancy! I didn't mean—"

Don jumped up, too. The boat lurched again, and Nancy pitched over the side into the cold, dirty water.

Chapter

Eleven

Nancy hit the water face first and went under. She gasped in shock—and inhaled a mouthful of slimy water. Coughing and choking, she struggled to get herself upright and expel the water.

"Stop the boat!" Don yelled frantically.

"Hey! Man overboard! I mean, girl overboard!" bellowed a guy with a big laugh. "Throw her a life jacket or something!"

But the boat kept moving through the tunnel. "I'm coming, Nancy!" Don called.

Just as Nancy had gotten to her feet, Don jumped into the water beside her.

"Ow!" he yelped in surprise. "I thought it was deeper than this."

Nancy was still trying to catch her breath. She pushed her streaming hair out of her face. "It can't be any deeper than five feet or so," she gasped, coughing again. "But this water is filthy. I hope we don't get sick."

"Nancy, I'm so sorry," Don said. "I didn't mean to scare you. I was just so mad when I realized what you were thinking—but really, you've got to believe me. I'm not the guy you're looking for." He sighed. "In more ways than one, I guess."

"Lovers overboard!" bellowed the guy on the boat before Nancy could answer. "Drowned in the name of loooooove!" His laughter died away as the boat rounded a corner and vanished from sight.

Nancy and Don were left staring at each other in the dim light. "I'm sorry, too, Don," Nancy said. "I shouldn't have panicked. I *knew* you weren't the kind of guy to do something like this. I guess I just didn't trust my own feelings."

It was true. She'd realized the minute she hit the water that she was being silly.

"Let's talk about it later, though," Nancy continued. "We'd better get out of here before the next boat comes along."

They turned toward the exit and began wading through the water.

"Boy, are we going to mess up your car," Don said as they slogged their way out.

"Oh, well. It's seen worse." She couldn't remember when, though.

After a couple of minutes they reached the exit. Unfortunately, there was no way they could get out of the water inconspicuously. About twenty grinning faces were waiting for them to arrive, and when they finally did appear everyone burst into hoots and applause.

Everyone except the guy who was in charge of the ride. "What do you dumb kids think this is, the beach?" he yelled when they'd pulled themselves out of the water. "You're not supposed to swim in there! I could get in a lot of trouble for this!"

"It was my fault," Don said quickly. "She didn't have anything to do with it. There was just a little—misunderstanding."

"You trying to tell me you pushed her in?"

"Don, can we please just go home instead of standing here dripping?" Nancy asked abruptly. "The parking lot's right over there, and I think I'll be sick if I don't get a shower pretty soon."

"What do you mean, sick?" the man in charge of the ride said. "There's nothing wrong with that water! You could drink it for breakfast!"

"Sure you could," Don snapped. "If you wanted to turn into a—"

"Don, let's *go.*" Nancy took his arm and

dragged him away. As they headed toward the parking lot they could still hear the man at the tunnel shouting at them.

Nancy looked over at Don. He was grinning, and at the sight she couldn't stop a smile from spreading across her own face. In a second they were both doubled up with laughter.

"This is the last time I let a date decide where we're going," Don said. "It's too dangerous. From now on I'm sticking to Pizza Palace. At least you know what to expect there."

"It hasn't been much of an evening for you, has it?" said Nancy as they reached her car. She took a blanket out of the trunk and spread it carefully across the front seat. She didn't want to spread any more of that horrible water around than she had to. "First I call you a crook, then I practically drown you. Well"—she smiled mischievously—"I *told* you when I first saw you at the party that I didn't want to get serious. Maybe next time you'll believe me."

"Oh, I will. Who knows how you'll try to convince me another time?"

Now that Nancy knew Don wasn't going to try to get her to go out with him anymore, she suddenly felt at ease with him again. She just wished he had proof of his innocence.

"You know, I've got an alibi, anyway," Don said, as if he'd read her mind. "At least I think I do—if you'll take my father's word for it. That time I saw you yesterday was the only time I left the house all day. I was showing my dad how to computerize the household accounts." He chuckled. "I'm still not sure he understands how to do it, but he'll vouch for my having been there."

"That's good to hear," Nancy said. And she meant it.

"Can we stop at my house before I take you home?" she asked Don as they reached the outskirts of her neighborhood. "I know this sounds awfully businesslike, but I'd like to check the phone machine and see if there are any messages. This isn't the kind of case that shuts down at the end of the day."

"That's fine," Don said. "I'm in no hurry. I can even wait downstairs if you want to take a shower and change. You got a lot more of that gunk on you than I did."

But when she turned onto her street, Nancy realized that she wasn't going to get that shower after all. Not for a while, anyway.

Ned's car was parked in the driveway. As her headlights lit up the front of the house, Nancy saw Ned sitting on the front porch. And he didn't look happy. He jumped to his feet and stalked toward them when he saw them.

"Uh-oh. You'd better wait in the car," Nancy told Don nervously as she turned off the ignition.

"No way!" he protested. "I'm going to tell him

you didn't do anything wrong. Hey, Ned," he called as he got out of the car. "This wasn't a date, you know. Nancy was just—"

"I'm not interested in what you have to say, Cameron." Nancy had never seen Ned so angry. "I want to talk to Nancy. Now."

Nancy took a deep breath to make sure her voice wouldn't shake. "Well, you'll have to wait for a little while, Ned. Let me take Don home first, okay?"

"Fine." Ned bit out the word. "But I'm coming with you."

"Good," Nancy said, as composed as she could be. "Then we'll have a chance to explain everything to you."

But it looked as though Ned wasn't going to give them a chance to explain anything. "Why don't you leave Nancy alone, Cameron?" he asked the minute they were all in the car. "What does it take to show you she's not interested?"

"Look, Ned, I—" Don began.

"Save it," Ned snapped. "I don't want to hear it."

"Ned, will you just listen for one second?" Nancy asked. "Don and I *weren't* out on a date. We went out so I could talk to him about the case."

"She's right, Ned," Don said. He gave a short laugh. "She thinks of me as a suspect—nothing more."

"No, no! I know you're not guilty now," Nancy interposed. "But I didn't know that until this evening, Ned. So now we can all relax. Okay?" Ned was silent. *"Okay?"* Nancy asked.

"Okay," Ned said at last. "Sorry if I went overboard. Wait, what's so funny?"

"You're not the one who went overboard," Nancy told him.

"What are you talking about?" Ned asked. "Come to think of it, you guys do look sort of wet. What happened?"

"Nancy can fill you in on that later," Don said. "Here's my street."

Suddenly his voice grew sharp. "Hey, what's going on at my house? My parents are supposed to be out this evening."

Don's house was at the end of the block. Except for the light on the front porch, it was completely dark.

But as they moved closer they saw a light flickering inside. It moved from one room to another, passing from the front of the house to the back.

Then, when they were just in front of the house, they saw the dark silhouette of someone stealing past a window.

"Don! There's a burglar in there!" Nancy gasped.

Chapter

Twelve

Nancy was out of the car and racing up Don's walk before she'd even fully decided what she was going to do. Don and Ned were close behind.

"Who's there?" Nancy shouted as she reached the front door, which was slightly ajar. "What are you doing in there?"

Slam!

"That's the back door! He's getting out the back way!" Don yelled. "If we run, maybe we can cut him off!"

Together he and Ned rushed around the side of the house. Nancy held back, waiting to see whether they'd chase anyone to the front. She could hear them crashing around in the yard, but there was no sign of any intruder. Was it possible he—or she—was still in the house?

Cautiously Nancy inched the front door open. Swinging free, it creaked a little on its hinges. Nancy peered in.

It would be crazy to walk in there, she told herself. She shivered. What if someone was watching her from inside, waiting for her to make a move?

Nancy reached around the door until she was touching the wall. She slid her hand along it. There had to be a light switch somewhere—

"Nancy? Is that you?" It was a raspy voice behind her.

Nancy whirled around. Someone was staggering slowly toward her, and as the figure drew closer she was able to make out who it was.

"Patrick!" she cried. "What's happened to you? Ned! Don! Come here!"

Patrick Emmons, his nose bleeding, his shirt half torn off, took one more wobbly step—and collapsed.

Nancy rushed over to kneel beside him. He was speaking so faintly she could hardly hear him.

"Be all right in a minute . . ." he murmured. "Just had the—wind knocked out of me. I'm— really okay."

In a minute he sat up. "That's better," he said, still rather groggy. He shook his head as if to clear it. "I just collided with a guy in a very big hurry."

"Who was it? Where?" Don asked urgently.

"Right there—two houses down." Patrick pointed. "I was taking a walk." He lived on the next street over from Don's, Nancy knew. "I guess *he* was just taking a run. He ran right into me and knocked me down. He didn't even stop to see how I was."

"Which way did he go?" asked Nancy. Patrick pointed down the road.

"Come on, Ned! Let's see if we can catch him!" Don said. He and Ned tore down the block.

"Who was it?" Patrick asked. "A friend of theirs? What was he running from?"

"We saw a burglar in Don's house," Nancy answered. "When we got to the front door, he ran out the back. He must have banged into you while he was running away."

"*Another* burglar?" Patrick sounded bewildered. "That's kind of a weird coincidence, isn't it?"

"I don't think it's a coincidence. I don't think it was *another* burglar, either." Nancy's mouth was drawn tight. "Want to come in with me and see what he's done this time?"

"I guess so," Patrick said in a resigned voice.

Cautiously they stepped inside, and Nancy switched on the hall light.

"Are you sure someone's been in here?" Patrick whispered.

Nancy remembered Don's house fairly well from the times she had visited him in high school. She didn't know what kind of damage she was expecting—but she hadn't been expecting no damage at all. The whole downstairs looked neat and untouched. A vase of dried flowers was perched precariously on the edge of the piano in the living room—but it hadn't fallen. The TV, VCR, and stereo system were all in place in the den. The silver candlesticks in the dining room still stood on the sideboard.

Puzzled, Nancy walked up the stairs with Patrick at her heels. The master bedroom was as neat as the downstairs. Don's brother's room was a mess, but just an ordinary mess, the kind any sixteen-year-old boy would make. A tiger cat was sleeping in a pile of clothes in the corner. It opened one eye lazily as Nancy walked through the room.

"I wish you could tell us what's been going on here, little guy," she said. But the cat just closed its eye and snuggled back down.

Then Nancy and Patrick walked into Don's room—and stopped short. So *this* had been the intruder's target.

All the drawers in the bureau had been dumped onto the floor, and ink poured over their contents. Books had been yanked out of the bookcases, and their pages ripped out. The mirror was smashed. The bed was dripping with after-shave. And all Don's athletic trophies had been pounded shapeless with a fireplace poker. The poker was still lying beside the pile of dented metal, but Nancy was sure there wouldn't be any fingerprints on it. If this was the same guy who had attacked Monica's and Wendy's houses, he would have been too careful to leave prints.

As she looked around the trashed room Nancy felt sick. *This* was only a form of revenge against Don. All the intruder had wanted to do was get him.

Poor Don, she thought. What a night he's had.

That reminded her of something. "Patrick, you were pretty sure Don was the guy behind all these attacks," she said. "I know now that there's absolutely no way he could have been involved. He's even got an alibi for the times both robberies were committed yesterday. What made you suspect him?"

"I didn't say I *suspected* him." Patrick sounded shocked. "It was just a—well, a speculation. You must have blown up what I said into something bigger."

"But you said—" Nancy searched her memory

for his exact words. "Oh, no," she said. "Then that means I put Don through all this for nothing."

Patrick was staring at her. "All what?" he asked. "You mean you—you accused him?"

"Practically," Nancy said. "Boy, do I feel—" But before she could go on, she heard Don's voice.

"Nancy? Are you up there?"

"Yes, I am," she called down. "So's Patrick. You'd better come up and see your room, Don."

Don came pounding up the stairs, Ned behind him. "We ran about four blocks, but we didn't see— Oh, no . . ." His voice trailed off in horror.

"Oh, yes," Nancy said. "Whoever it was doesn't seem to have overlooked anything. And this is the only room he touched. Don, do you know anyone who has this kind of grudge against you?"

Don had gone over to the pathetic heap of bashed-up trophies. He was holding one now, turning it over and over as though he could somehow restore it with his bare hands. When he finally answered, he sounded like a sleepwalker.

"Of course I don't. I mean, I don't get along with everybody, but—I'm just a regular guy! What could I have done that was bad enough to make someone hate me this much?"

"Don't blame yourself. It may not be anything you've done," Nancy said quickly. "Whoever this is has a grudge against a lot of people. I just wondered if any names might pop into your head, that's all."

Her list of suspects seemed to be growing bigger and smaller at the same time. Today she'd added Don to the list, but now he was definitely off it again. That meant she'd have to add someone else—but who?

Or *would* she have to add someone else? She'd been sure Judd was guilty before she began investigating Don. With Don's name cleared, wasn't it possible that Judd was in the running again?

"Could you see the guy who knocked you down at all?" she asked Patrick.

He shook his head. "It was too dark. All I noticed was that he was wearing a leather jacket. I felt it when he banged into me."

A leather jacket. Judd did have a leather jacket. Of course, so did hundreds of guys in River Heights. The jacket alone didn't prove anything.

But it certainly didn't make Judd look any less guilty, either.

Suddenly Nancy noticed that Patrick was staring at her strangely. "Nancy, I don't mean to get personal," he said, "but you look kind of messed up yourself. Did you fall down or something?"

"Fall down? Oh!" Suddenly Nancy remembered the Tunnel of Love. The past hour had driven it out of her head entirely. Her clothes had dried out a little, but now she realized how awful she must look.

She giggled. "I guess you could say that. Or maybe it would be more exact to say I fell out."

"Out of what?" Patrick and Ned asked in unison.

Don spoke up. "Nancy, I can straighten things up here. Why don't you go home and fill Ned in? Then take a six-hour shower and go to bed. No, I'll manage," he said when Nancy opened her mouth to protest. "There's not that much to do, anyway. It's only—it's only trophies and things. . . . " His voice trailed off again as he looked around the room.

"I'll help you clean up," Patrick said. "We'll have the place back to normal in no time. You *should* go home, Nancy. I'm sure you're not planning to sleep in tomorrow."

Nancy winced. "Not likely. Not until I find out who this crackpot is. Well, Don, if you're really sure—"

"Yes," he said firmly.

"Then Ned and I *will* take off. I'll talk to both of you first thing tomorrow. And, Don, I'm really sorry. About everything."

On the drive back to her house, Nancy told Ned how she had fallen into the water, and when he finally stopped laughing, he was properly sympathetic.

Now they were standing by her front door. "You'd better not kiss me good night," Nancy told Ned. "Whatever was in that water might be catching. I'd love to ask you in," she went on, "but—I've got to be honest—all I can think about is taking a shower."

"Well, as long as you're not thinking about Don—or anyone else. It's late, anyway. I should be getting home." Ned gave her a gingerly pat on the cheek. *"That* probably won't give me typhoid," he said.

Nancy smiled. "I don't think so. And I'll take a rain check on that kiss, if you don't mind."

"No problem. Want to do something tomorrow night? If you're not busy putting people in jail, I mean?"

"Well, Mr. Nickerson, I'm a busy, busy girl. But I think I can manage to squeeze in some time for you."

"Good." Ned touched her cheek again. "I'm glad we straightened everything out," he whispered.

"Me, too," Nancy said, and she blew him a kiss. "Thanks for being so understanding, Ned. I'll see you tomorrow—and I'll be *clean.*"

The minute his car pulled out of the driveway she bolted up the stairs and turned on the shower.

After twenty luxurious minutes—and three shampoos—Nancy decided she'd finally washed out every trace of slime and dirt. Now all she had to do was throw her T-shirt and skirt into the wash and get ready for bed.

Nancy was almost asleep before her head hit the pillow. But it was only an hour later that something jarred her awake. She sat up, her heart pounding.

Oh! she thought groggily. It's just the phone. It must have been ringing for a long time.

Who could be calling so late? Nancy groaned and reached over to her bedside table.

She cleared her throat and picked up the receiver. "Hello?" she said as alertly as she could.

"Nancy!" The voice at the other end was a sobbing scream.

"It's Wendy. Nancy, he's found me. And he's going to kill me!"

Chapter

Thirteen

INSTANTLY NANCY SNAPPED wide-awake. "Who's going to kill you? Is there someone in the house?" she asked.

"N-no," Wendy stammered. "But someone's been calling me. At first I thought it was a joke—maybe a friend or something—because whoever it was just kept laughing and hanging up. But then it got awful. He said—he said—he said he knew all about me. He knew everything I was doing. His voice—he sounded like someone in a horror movie. And a couple of minutes ago he called and said he was coming over to kill me!"

"Wendy, I'm putting on my clothes now," Nancy said. "I'll be over as fast as I can. When I get to your house I'll knock three times loudly and three times softly. *Don't open the door* unless you hear that knock. Okay? And, Wendy, you've got to call the police—now!"

"I can't," Wendy said tearfully. "I just can't involve them. Please hurry, Nancy. I can't stand being alone here."

Nancy hung up the phone, threw on a pair of jeans and a T-shirt, and raced downstairs. Her sandals were at the foot of the stairs. She picked them up and carried them out to the car with her. With a roar the Mustang jumped to life, and she backed out of the driveway.

It was 1:15 A.M. by the car clock. "At least the roads are clear," Nancy muttered. She was free to drive as fast as she safely could—and it seemed like only seconds before she was pulling up in front of Wendy's huge house.

It was completely dark.

"Oh, no," Nancy whispered. Had the attacker gotten there before her?

Her heart was thudding as she walked up to the front door and knocked. Three times loudly, three times softly. Then silence.

Nancy repeated the knock, and this time she heard a tiny creak. Someone was lifting the mail slot.

"Nancy? Is that you?" came a timid whisper through the slot.

"Yes, it is," she whispered back.

Slowly the door swung open. Then Wendy grabbed Nancy's hand and pulled her inside.

"I'm so glad it's you!" she gasped. "I kept thinking I heard someone breaking in!"

Well, Nancy thought grimly, that might very well be happening. "Where was the sound coming from?" she asked.

"Out back. I know it's probably nothing, but—"

"Let's go see," Nancy said. "Which way's the back door?"

"Right through here—ouch!" Suddenly Nancy heard a crash. Some small piece of furniture skittered across the floor, and Wendy started hopping up and down. "Ouch! Ouch! Oh, my shin!" Wendy moaned. "I didn't see that footstool!"

"Why are the lights off, anyway?" Nancy asked.

"I *turned* them off. I didn't want that guy to be able to see where I was!"

"Well, I think they should be turned back on," Nancy said. "People are less likely to break in if they think someone's home. And turning the lights on now would help scare off a prowler. Where's the switch?"

"I'll get it." Just having something to do calmed Wendy down. "The back door's right through the kitchen," she continued briskly, leading Nancy to it.

"Well, I can't imagine *any* prowler who'd be dumb enough to hang around when we're out here," she told Wendy cheerfully, "but let me just have a look." She stepped outside and threw on the floodlights.

No one appeared to be lurking behind any of the trees. No one was crouched in back of the brick barbecue grill. No one was hiding in the changing house next to the swimming pool. If anyone had been trying to break in, he was gone now.

Back in the kitchen, the phone rang.

"Oh, no. It's him again!" Wendy whimpered. "Can't we just ignore it?"

"Don't worry," Nancy said. "I'll answer it this time." She pulled the back door shut. "You bolt the door."

In the black-tiled kitchen, the phone's ringing echoed, jarring Nancy.

"Hello?" she said crisply.

There was a pause. Then a hollow chuckle and a horribly distorted, cackling voice.

"You'd better get out of there if you know what's good for you—*Nancy Drew!*"

Click! Whoever was calling had hung up.

And whoever it was knew who *she* was. That meant he'd been following her movements that night. Maybe he was calling to threaten Nancy now!

Wendy was hovering nervously in the doorway. "Was it him?" she whispered.

Nancy nodded. "But this time I think he was looking for me."

"Looking for you!" Wendy's eyes grew enormous. "But that means—"

"Exactly," Nancy broke in. "Hang on, Wendy. Let me think a minute. There was something familiar about the background noise, but I can't put my finger on it. Wherever that guy was calling from was a place I've been recently. Now where was it?"

Suddenly it came to her. Judd's garage— the only place Nancy knew where loud soft-rock ballads could be heard in the middle of the night.

"Okay. Now it's my turn to make a few calls," Nancy told Wendy. "I've got to get over to the Church Street Garage. Want to come?"

"Are you kidding? You think I'd stay here alone?"

It was 2:00 A.M. Sorry, Ned, Nancy thought as she dialed his number.

"Sorry to call you so late, Ned," she said when he finally answered. "I was just wondering if you'd mind switching our date for tomorrow night to tonight. Right now."

"You're not kidding, are you?" Ned answered with a yawn.

"I wish I were. I think I've managed to track down our prowler. He may be at the Church Street Garage. Wendy and I are about to head over there, but I think we may need reinforcements. Can you meet us?"

"Sure thing," Ned answered. He sounded more wide-awake now. "Ten minutes?"

"Great. Thanks a whole lot, Ned."

Getting George up was a little harder. When Nancy had finished explaining everything, George groaned, "Of course, Nan. Anything for you," and went right back to sleep. Nancy had to shout her name over and over before George woke up again. By then she'd forgotten everything Nancy had just told her. Nancy hoped she would have better luck with Bess.

Wendy came back into the kitchen just as Nancy was hanging up from Bess. "Okay, let's go," Nancy said.

Wendy took a deep breath. "I'm ready. But Nancy, one thing—"

"Yes?"

"Don't you want to put on your sandals? You've been carrying them around all this time."

* * *

"Are you sure there's someone in there? Why would a garage be open at this time of night?" whispered George.

"Well, I'm not sure it's open—but I *am* sure that this is where that call was coming from," Nancy whispered back.

Nancy, George, Bess, Ned, and Wendy were all huddled in the parking lot across the street from the Church Street Garage. The music had finally been shut off, and the night was dead silent.

Nancy was feeling very edgy. No one lived in this neighborhood; it was just a strip of fast-food restaurants, garages, and other daytime businesses. No cars ever came to this section of town at night, and there was a lost, deserted quality to the streets. Bess kept yawning and rubbing her eyes, and it was obvious that George thought Nancy had dragged them out on a wild-goose chase.

"All right, I admit we'll look stupid trying to get in if there's no one there," Nancy said, "but we'll look even stupider if we all go home and it turns out I was right. Let's get over there."

"Are we all going in together?" asked Ned.

"I think it would make more sense if I go in while the rest of you stake out the exits," Nancy answered. "I know there's one exit out back—I saw it right behind Judd's office—and there's another on the side. Ned, you take the back, and

George can take the side. And of course there's the one in front. Why don't you take that one, Bess?" She didn't want to say it, but she thought the front door would be the safest for Bess. If Judd wanted to escape, it wasn't likely he'd do it through the front. Nancy was sure that either Ned or George could handle Judd if he tried to get by them.

"Wendy and I will go in by the back door," she said. "I can pick the lock if I have to."

But as it turned out, she didn't have to. The door wasn't locked. "Stay right behind me, Wendy," Nancy murmured as she stepped inside.

Judd's office looked as though he'd been working late. The radio was on, tuned to an all-night soft-rock station. There were papers all over his desk, along with a half-full Styrofoam cup of coffee and a doughnut with a bite out of it.

Something about the hominess of the scene was wrong. It was too pat. Was this the desk of someone who'd been making threatening phone calls all night?

It was all starting to seem stranger and stranger —and yet Nancy knew in her bones that she hadn't been mistaken about where the calls were coming from.

As she and Wendy crept into the garage's main work area, Nancy realized that she was afraid. Not afraid of catching Judd. Afraid that something terrible had happened here.

There was no one in the other two offices, and no sign that anyone had been there recently. The employees' bathroom was empty, but Nancy saw that someone had forgotten to turn off the cold-water tap.

Or maybe that person just hadn't bothered. Nancy took a closer look at the sink.

The bar of soap was stained with something red. There were traces of red on the white porcelain of the sink. And the crumpled-up paper towels in the wastebasket were drenched with dark red.

Blood. Someone had been attacked in this garage. And perhaps not very long ago.

Nancy ran into the garage's main work area. Wendy was behind her—but it was Wendy who screamed at what they saw.

Judd Reese was lying unconscious in the pit under the hydraulic press. And it looked as though someone had bashed him over the head!

Chapter

Fourteen

ALL RIGHT. WE'LL be waiting for you here."

Slowly Nancy hung up the phone in Judd's office. For the second time in forty-eight hours she was waiting for an ambulance. But she hadn't been nearly so worried about Celia as she was about Judd.

She didn't dare touch Judd's head, but it looked as though he'd lost a lot of blood. And it took a long time for her to find his pulse. Judd's attacker definitely meant business.

The night air was warm, but Nancy shivered. Whoever was behind all this had just upped the ante. Where was it all going to stop?

She walked back out into the main garage, where Ned, Bess, George, and Wendy were standing around Judd.

"The ambulance is on its way," she said. "But there's no reason for all of you to wait. Why don't you go home? I can stay here until they come. Maybe one of you could give Wendy a ride home."

"Uh, Nancy, maybe I could stay here with you?" said Wendy. "I just can't stand the thought of going back to that empty house."

"Of course you can't. I should have thought of that," agreed Nancy. "Do you want to spend the rest of the night at my house?"

Wendy looked incredibly relieved. "Thank you," she said fervently. "I'd really appreciate that."

"But of course we're not leaving the two of you alone here, Nan," said George. Ned and Bess nodded their agreement. "We don't need our sleep *that* badly. "We'll all wait together. I'm sorry I didn't believe you, by the way. You were right, as usual."

"Oh, don't worry," Nancy said. "I know it's not easy to get out of bed and come to some garage at two in the morning. Anyway, we'll be fine here."

A couple of minutes later the ambulance pulled up. As she watched the paramedics load

Judd swiftly onto the stretcher, Nancy asked, "Can you get any idea of when he was attacked?"

"Well," one of the paramedics said, "it's hard to be exact, of course, but I'd say it was about an hour ago, judging by the way the blood's clotted. Maybe more. He looks as though he's been unconscious for a while."

An hour ago. It was hard to believe, but less than an hour had passed since Nancy had gotten the phone call from the garage. If Judd had been attacked *more* than an hour ago, that meant he couldn't possibly have been the one who made the call. He, too, was off the suspects' list. If she hadn't been so worried about him, Nancy would have been delighted.

"Have you gotten in touch with his relatives?" the same paramedic was asking. "They'd better be notified as soon as possible."

Nancy could feel herself blushing. "I—I'm afraid I don't know who they are."

"I do," said Wendy. "His parents live on Calhoun Street. Do you want me to call them, Nancy?"

"That'd be great."

When Wendy hung up, she looked tired and drained. "They're heading right over to the hospital," she said. "I gave them your number and told them to call when they know how he's doing. I hope that was okay." Wendy sighed. "I feel so bad. Here I was complaining about a few phone calls and having my VCR taken. What's that compared to something like this?"

"I know." At least there was one good thing about this case, Nancy thought to herself. It was forcing Wendy to be a little more caring. Nancy hoped the change would be permanent. "Whoever's making these attacks is getting madder," Nancy continued. "Maybe Judd will be able to tell us who it was—if he recovers enough."

Both girls were quiet on the drive back to Nancy's house. "Do you think you'll have any trouble getting to sleep?" Nancy asked Wendy as they made up the spare bed. "Want some cocoa or something?"

"No, thanks." Wendy yawned hugely. "We've been through a lot tonight, and it would take an earthquake to keep me awake now."

Nancy was exhausted, too. She didn't even bother taking off her clothes. For the second time that night she fell asleep as soon as her head hit the pillow. And for the second time the telephone jarred her awake after what seemed like only a few minutes.

"Oh, no," she groaned as she reached blindly out of bed. "This case is nothing *but* phone calls."

After fumbling around for a few seconds, she finally found the receiver. "Hello?" she asked groggily.

"Nancy, it's Patrick." He was whispering tensely. "There's someone outside my house. I can hear him. And I think I know who it is. It's— Wait! He's coming in!"

Suddenly Nancy heard a terrible crash—and then a moan of pain.

"Patrick! Patrick, are you there?"

But now all she heard was a muffled shout, and a crack as if Patrick had dropped the receiver. Then the line went dead.

Nancy rushed into Wendy's room and shook her awake. "Wendy, there's something going on at Patrick's. I've got to get over there right now."

"Uh-huh," Wendy yawned, burrowing her face deeper into the pillow.

"Wendy! Did you hear me?"

"Sure, Nancy. Okay, good night. . . ." Her voice trailed off into a wordless murmur.

"Oh, no," Nancy said aloud. She'd just have to leave Wendy here.

Nancy rushed downstairs and out to the car. "Oh, please," she said aloud as she drove along through the dark streets. "Don't let anything have happened to Patrick. I hope his parents aren't in danger, but why didn't I hear them trying to help him? Enough people have been hurt already."

Nancy felt an eternity pass before she arrived at the cozy house. She parked the car and rushed up to the front door. It was locked—no surprise. She pounded on the door, then rapped the shiny brass knocker as hard as she could. A light went on in the house next door, and a sleepy face peered out at her from the next-door kitchen window. But no one came to the door at Patrick's house.

Then she suddenly heard an upstairs window slide open. "Who's there?" a woman called down in a low voice.

"It's Nancy Drew," Nancy called up softly. "I'm a friend of Patrick's from high school. Please let me in. I just got a call from him. I think he was attacked!"

"Oh, no! *Patrick!*" the woman said frantically, and then Nancy heard feet running down the stairs.

In a second the front door burst open. Mrs. Emmons—a slim, middle-aged woman—was standing there. Behind her stood Patrick's father, a burly man who was still rubbing his eyes. Both of them were in their bathrobes. Both looked fearful—and bewildered.

"He—he doesn't seem to be at home," Mr. Emmons said. "Where could he be?"

"You didn't hear him yelling?" Nancy asked incredulously.

"N-no," said Patrick's father. "Was he yelling?"

What was going on here? "Have you checked his room?" Nancy said. She walked into the house as the Emmonses stepped aside.

"No," said Mrs. Emmons, "but he would have heard me call out for him if he was in there. Wait! Where are you going?"

Nancy was already heading up the stairs. "His room's up here?" she asked.

"Well, yes, but I'm sure he's not in there—" Patrick's mother began.

"He's not," Nancy said flatly from the top of the stairs. "But *someone's* been here. And I think Patrick was calling me to tell me who it was."

Mrs. Emmons gave a low moan when she saw her son's room, but the sight inside was all too familiar to Nancy. The room was destroyed—books ripped apart, records taken out of their sleeves and broken in half, clothes and papers covered with ink. It was a virtual repeat of the damage done earlier to Don's and Monica's rooms.

But there was something different. What was it? Nancy wondered.

She turned to Patrick's parents. "This is very strange," she said. "I know Patrick said he was calling from home. I don't see how you could have missed hearing whoever did this!"

"Well, we didn't hear a thing," said Mr. Emmons blankly. "He needed to think some things over, he said. He told us he was going for a drive, and we went to bed before he got back. I didn't hear him come in. I can't imagine where he is."

Nancy scanned the torn-up room again. "Does it look as if anything's missing from this room? Anything valuable, I mean?"

Mrs. Emmons looked around the room, her face strained and anxious.

"Not—not that I can see," she said. "A couple of the trophies are made of silver, but even they're still here."

The trophies! That was what was different. The trophies in Don's room had been destroyed along with everything else, but Patrick's shone brightly from the rack against the wall.

Why? Nancy asked herself. But Mrs. Emmons was speaking again. "Of course Patrick had his more valuable things—like his stereo—at school with him," she said. "I think he sold most of that stuff when he came back here."

When he came back here?

"Wait a minute. I think I'm missing something," Nancy said. "What do you mean, he came back? Doesn't he go back to college in a couple of days?"

Now both of Patrick's parents looked confused. "You—you don't know?" his father asked.

"Don't know what?"

Patrick's mother let out a long, shaky breath. "He must have been too ashamed to tell his friends. Patrick was expelled from school last semester. He's not going back." Sudden tears filled her eyes, and she turned her head away to hide them. Her husband put his arm around her.

Nancy couldn't believe what she was hearing. Patrick expelled? But he'd just told her he was about to return there!

"Patrick's such a good boy," Mrs. Emmons said loyally. "He just had a terrible year there, that's all. The work was so much harder than he'd expected—and then when he was cut from the football team— Well, it just seemed as though everything collapsed around him. He hasn't really been the same since. But I—I know that he'll get back on track soon."

"Of course he will," said Mr. Emmons. "He's never let us down before—" He broke off and peered at Nancy. "Are you all right?"

"Cut from the football team?" Nancy asked slowly. "But I thought—"

He'd been cut from the team. He'd had trouble with his schoolwork. That meant Patrick had been lying all along.

What else had he been lying about?

"I can see you're surprised," Mr. Emmons went on. "I guess Patrick just couldn't bring himself to tell his friends. He's so competitive—and he's always been so proud."

"I know he has," Nancy said. Unconsciously her eyes moved to the rack of gleaming trophies that hadn't been disturbed by the intruder.

Now a suspicion flowered full-blown in Nancy's mind, and she couldn't get rid of it. The conclusion was inescapable.

Patrick had to have staged this "robbery" himself. But he had been unable to destroy the things he was most proud of.

Patrick was the culprit. She'd guessed that revenge lay behind these crimes, and she was right.

Patrick was striking back at whoever had been more successful than he: Monica, with her budding acting career; Celia, who'd made herself beautiful; Judd, who was finally turning his life around; Don, who was working hard at college in a way Patrick obviously hadn't; and Wendy, his old girlfriend, who'd found a new boyfriend and managed perfectly well without Patrick.

But where was Patrick now?

Nancy's mind was racing. Each time Patrick had plundered a new place, he'd done something to lure Nancy away from the scene first. If he'd called her to his house—and then disappeared—it must have been a ploy to get her away from the next place he planned to visit.

What if the next place was her own house—

with Wendy inside, all alone? If Patrick was the culprit, then he was the one who had been terrifying Wendy with those phone calls. And that meant—

"He's going over there to kill her!" Nancy gasped.

Chapter

Fifteen

"Mr. and Mrs. Emmons, I've got to go," Nancy said abruptly. "I'm awfully sorry about all of this, but perhaps you should call the police."

Patrick's parents were staring at her. "What's going on? Is Patrick all right?" asked his mother.

"I'm afraid not, but I can't explain right now," Nancy answered.

"He's been hurt!" Mrs. Emmons gasped.

"I don't think he's been hurt, Mrs. Emmons," Nancy said gently. "I just think Patrick played a few 'pranks,' and now he's in over his head. I'm so sorry," Nancy said again, then she rushed downstairs and out to her car.

When she reached her own house it looked reassuringly normal—so normal that Nancy felt a momentary qualm. Had she made a terrible mistake? Had she gotten Mrs. Emmons all upset for nothing?

The lights were on downstairs in the living room. Wendy must have come down. Nancy peeked into the living room window and smiled. Wendy was curled up on the sofa watching TV. She had obviously calmed down after Nancy left!

Nancy unlocked the front door and rushed in. "Oh, thank heaven, you're all right!" she called from the front hall as she ran toward the living room. "I was so afraid Patrick was coming over here—"

"Nancy. He was here, but I think he left." Wendy's voice was a tiny thread of its usual self. "Help me."

Nancy rushed into the living room.

"Help me," Wendy begged again. She couldn't even turn around to look at Nancy.

She'd been tied hand and foot to the sofa.

"He made me get comfortable before he tied me," Wendy whispered. "He wanted to make sure I'd look normal so you wouldn't be scared to come inside."

"Oh, Wendy!" Nancy was already working on the knots. Wendy had been tied up with clothesline, and it must have hurt terribly. There were red welts all over her wrists as Nancy untied them. "But where is he now?" she asked Wendy.

"Waiting for you, Nancy. Why don't you just have a seat?"

The voice, light and pleasant, came from behind her.

Nancy whirled around. Patrick was standing in the doorway. There was a broad grin on his face, another roll of clothesline looped around his arm—and a pistol in his hand.

"You're wasting your time untying her. Neither of you is going anywhere."

Still training the gun on both girls, Patrick walked over to an armchair next to the sofa and plunked himself down. "Really, Nancy, I meant it—sit down," he said, waving the gun casually in the air. "Let's just reminisce about the old days, shall we?"

"What's there to reminisce about?" Nancy asked in as casual a voice as she could manage. "It's not that long ago." Wendy was looking at her as though she were out of her mind, but Nancy was hoping she could get Patrick to talk. If she could, she might be able to distract him— and get the gun away from him.

"Remember when we were all so happy together?" Patrick asked. "Especially Wendy and me.

Although I don't expect you can remember that far back, Wendy. You've gone on to better things, I know."

Now Wendy looked indignant. She struggled to sit upright on the sofa, but it was no use—she had to flop back down again. "Why are you mad at me, Patrick? *You* broke up with *me,* remember? How can you blame me?"

"I broke up with you because you weren't paying enough attention to me!" Patrick exploded. "You didn't care about me! All you thought about was cheerleading! You never had any time for me!" His voice had become an ugly whine.

"And you've never forgiven her," Nancy said quietly. "You wanted someone who'd devote every minute to you."

"Of course I did! I wanted someone who cared. That's the least a guy like me deserves, don't you think?"

"Oh, of course," Nancy said politely.

"Don't humor me!" Patrick shouted. "What did my mother tell you? Did you talk to her?"

"Yes, I did," answered Nancy. "I think you can guess what she told me, Patrick. That you wouldn't be going back to school."

"Not going back to school? But why not?" Wendy asked. She sounded as shocked as Nancy had felt when she'd heard the news.

Patrick thrust out his chin. "It was ridiculous there!" he said. *"No one* could survive that kind of competition. Why didn't someone warn me about it in high school? Around here I was popular and everything was easy, but in college the pressure never let up!"

"So you flunked out?" Nancy asked.

Patrick winced. "Well, that's probably what *they'd* call it. Not that there was anyone there who offered to help me get my grades back up. They just didn't care about me, I guess. But it was really more my football coach's fault. He just wouldn't let me play enough. If he'd kept me on the team I wouldn't have had so much extra time on my hands. You know what it's like when you get bored." He chuckled sheepishly, and for a chilling second he looked exactly like the sweet-faced, popular guy he'd been until just a couple of hours ago.

"I don't understand what you mean," Nancy said carefully. "Did you get in some other kind of trouble, too?"

Patrick gave an elaborate sigh. "No, I did not get in some other kind of trouble," he said, mimicking her. "I was just borrowing that stuff they caught me with. But try to explain that to the dean of students!"

Nancy didn't dare press Patrick too hard. There was no need for him to be more specific, anyway. It was obvious he'd screwed up in a major way at college—and just as obvious that he wanted other people to suffer with him.

He stood up suddenly. "Okay, enough reminiscing," he said. "Wendy, you're getting tied up again."

For a minute Nancy's hopes flared into life. How could Patrick tie Wendy and hold a gun at the same time? He'd have to put the gun down for a second, at least!

But Patrick just grinned at her as if he knew what she was thinking. "I'm not as stupid as you think I am," he said. "I'm going to make you tie her up, Nancy." He watched closely as Nancy retied Wendy's hands. Then he double-checked the knots while keeping the gun aimed at Nancy.

"Now, *you're* going to be a little more complicated, Nancy," Patrick continued when he'd finished with Wendy. "With your background and all, you probably know more tricks than she does. Let's see . . ." He stood for a minute, pondering. The gun he was pointing at Nancy never wavered.

"Why don't you go and stand in the corner with your face to the wall," Patrick suggested. "That way I can do your feet first. Don't think you can kick the gun out of my hands, either."

"I wouldn't dream of it," Nancy said, and she meant it. There might be time to think of an escape later, but for now she didn't dare do anything to provoke him.

So she just stood quietly while he tied her feet with more clothesline and then fastened her hands tightly behind her back. "Great!" he said when he was done. He gave her a friendly slap on the shoulder. "Now just stay put—not that you have much of a choice."

He walked to the center of the room. "I'm afraid I have to leave you lovely ladies now," he said. "I've still got so much to do. Thanks for everything."

"You're taking off?" Nancy asked.

"Yeah. It's time for me to get out of here." He started to walk slowly away—and then stopped.

"By the way, I'm going to make a stop in your garage first. I've got to get the stuff I need to burn this house down. With the two of you inside, of course."

Chapter

Sixteen

P ATRICK SAUNTERED OUT, whistling, and slammed
the front door behind him. Nancy heard him lock
it, and then she heard him opening the garage
door. Then all she could hear was a muffled
clanging as he started looking through the garage.

What would he find in there? Frantically Nancy tried to think. The barbecuing equipment?
Gasoline? Cleaning fluid? It would all be there,
she guessed. Nancy was sure that at any minute
he'd be back. . . .

Why didn't I call Bess or George or Ned before
I left for Patrick's house? she asked herself. Why

didn't I tell his parents where I was going? Someone could have been here by now! But Nancy knew that no one was coming to the rescue this time.

Wendy gave a stifled sob, and Nancy turned around. "He's going to roast us alive!" Wendy cried. "Can't you do something, Nancy?"

She'd have to try. "I'm going to get these ropes untied," Nancy said, "and then I'll untie you. We'll get out of here."

Or will we? she asked herself grimly. Patrick had tied her hands so tight that he'd cut off most of the circulation. Nancy could hardly move her fingers. Desperately she flexed her wrists, hoping to stretch the clothesline. It wouldn't budge.

"Hurry! Hurry!" Wendy begged in a shrieking whisper.

"I don't think I can— Wait! There we go!" At last the cord was giving a little. Nancy began twisting her wrists back and forth as hard as she could. They hurt so badly she wanted to scream, but she couldn't stop now. The cord was getting looser—looser. And finally Nancy slipped her swollen hands free.

"There!" she gasped, rubbing her bloodied wrists. "Now for the feet."

Untying her feet was easier, but it still took precious seconds to do it—seconds they didn't have. By the time Nancy had finally stepped out of the twisted coil of clothesline, the garage had become strangely silent. Was Patrick on his way back?

No time to think about that. Nancy rushed over to the sofa and began picking at the knots on Wendy's ankles. "There we go," she said at last. "Now sit up and rub your ankles. You've been tied up for so long that—"

Suddenly she froze. What was that noise?

A tiny click. The smallest sound imaginable, but Nancy knew instantly what it was. "He's coming in the door!" she whispered.

Wendy's face turned utterly white. "It's all over," she whispered. Nancy didn't answer. She couldn't. She knew Wendy was right.

Then the front door swished open, and Patrick strode back into the house.

"I thought so. You seem to have this mania for untying Wendy," he said coldly. He looked down reflectively at the gun in his hand. "Anyway, I couldn't find any gasoline, so I guess I'm just going to have to shoot you both."

He took a slow step toward them.

Nancy yelled, *"Run,* Wendy!" She tore up the front stairs with Wendy stumbling behind her.

A bullet whistled past Nancy's head and buried itself in the wall. Then another—and Wendy fell to the ground. "My feet!" she wailed. "I can't go fast!"

Nancy reached down, grabbed Wendy's bound hands, yanked her up the last two stairs, and dragged her behind one of the beds in the spare bedroom.

Silence.

Nancy silently untied Wendy as they listened to Patrick pace up the carpeted stairs.

Nancy's heart was hammering so fast it almost choked her. There was no way they could escape now. In a few seconds it would all be over.

Slowly Patrick's measured tread advanced toward them. Now he was halfway up—now two-thirds of the way. Now on the landing. "Come on, be sensible! You're just making it worse by trying to stall things," he sang out. "I know where you are."

Maybe he's just bluffing, Nancy thought feverishly. Oh, if only he is! He'd just started walking the wrong way down the hall. It was completely dark on the second floor, and maybe that would slow him down. If they could just manage to keep quiet, maybe he wouldn't find them.

But then Wendy scrambled to her feet and ran to the open window.

"Help!" she screamed at the top of her lungs. "Somebody, please help! He's going to kill us!"

"Shut up!" Patrick bellowed. With a muffled curse he thundered down the hall toward the spare room.

There was no time to think. Nancy had to stop him *now*.

She jumped to her feet and pressed herself into the wall by the doorway. The instant Patrick loomed into view, she scissored her leg up and caught him on the chin. He doubled up and fell to the ground without so much as a sigh.

The first pink light of dawn was creeping into the house when the police arrived and took Patrick away.

"How is Patrick doing now?" Monica Beckwith asked.

Nancy shook her head sadly. "Not great. This time there was no explaining away what he'd done. He couldn't take it and collapsed completely."

It was early the next evening. Nancy had accompanied the police to the station that morning when they'd booked Patrick.

After spending a couple of hours filling them in, she'd gone home to take a nap. She was still exhausted, but she was determined to wrap this case up once and for all. So she called all the people who had been involved in the case and invited them over to fill them in on what had happened—Wendy, Monica, Celia, Don, Ned, and of course Bess and George.

Only Judd wasn't there, but he was expected to

be leaving the hospital the next day. The blow to his head had given him temporary amnesia, and he still couldn't remember being attacked. Other than that, he was fine. Nancy had filled him in with a long talk on the phone that morning.

"Patrick says he planted the newspapers in your office when he brought his car in," she told Judd. "Didn't you see them there?"

Judd laughed. "If you really want to know the truth, it never occurred to me to keep tabs on my wastebasket. You're the detective, not me. I guess I should apologize," he added. "You *did* know what you were doing. And if it hadn't been for you, who knows when someone would have found me? I take back everything I said."

Now it was Nancy's turn to laugh. "Oh, you don't have to do that. I'm glad your memory's back. And I'm *really* glad you weren't guilty. Good luck with everything, Judd."

"So, Nan," George was saying now, "how did Patrick manage to figure out the timing on all those robberies and things?"

"Well, he *is* smart," Nancy said, "and once he'd established a pattern, it wasn't that hard for him. Wrecking Wendy's room at the beach house was probably the easiest, since all he had to do was go upstairs when no one was looking. He didn't even have to use the ladder the police were sure had been used—the marks it had made were probably there already. And then, of course, Patrick knew no one would suspect him when he'd been a victim, too."

"You mean he set up that trick with the charcoal starter himself?" Don asked in a startled voice.

"Yep."

Bess shuddered. "I don't know how *anyone* could go that far."

"And go that far twice, no less," Nancy said. "He practically had to beat himself up after he'd broken into Don's house, to make it look as though someone had banged into him."

"So Patrick came to the party planning to cause all that trouble?" Celia asked.

"Yes," Nancy replied. "He took a big gamble that no one would see him carry that stolen stuff out of the house."

"But no one would have suspected him—even if he'd carried the stuff out on his head," Monica said.

"I'm sure he could have come up with some kind of believable explanation."

"Still, it's amazing that no one saw him break into any of the houses," Ned observed.

"I know. He used the back door at Monica's and Wendy's, but still . . . I guess it was because he looked so squeaky clean that it never occurred to anyone that he was breaking in. Or maybe it was just beginner's luck—if you can call it that.

Once he had the stuff, he didn't even bother trying to find a good hiding place for it. The police found it under a tarp behind his parents' garage.

"Still, the stealing wasn't what Patrick was trying to do," Nancy went on. "He just wanted to get revenge on anyone doing better than he was. The attacks got more personal and nastier as he went along and got angrier."

Nancy shook her head. "And, boy, did I help him. He just followed me around. Then, when I'd go to investigate whatever clue he had dropped off for me, he'd be able to get into the place I'd just left."

She smiled ruefully at Don. "He kept pointing out how weird it was that you were on the scene so often. I never noticed that *he* was on the scene even more often."

"I still don't understand why he attacked Judd," Ned said. "Wasn't Judd your main suspect then? What was the point of getting him out of the way?"

"Well, he told the police he didn't plan to attack Judd at all," Nancy said. "He just wanted to use the phone there. For the privacy. But then he decided to make Judd seem even guiltier and turned on the radio, so I'd guess he was at the garage. But Judd caught him in the act, and Patrick picked up a crowbar and hit him over the head."

"This is all so creepy!" said Monica. "Poor Judd!" She shivered. "I guess I'm luckier than I thought. At least I didn't get hurt."

"Well, I did," said Celia, "but you know, I can't be as mad at Patrick as I should be now that I know the whole story. I mean, you can't help feeling sort of sorry for him."

Wendy had been pacing restlessly in front of the window for the last part of Nancy's explanation. Now she finally spoke. "I don't want to sound self-centered," she said haltingly, "but it does seem to me as if he was maybe trying to get at me a little more than everyone else—"

"You're absolutely right," said Nancy. "He's mad at all of us, but he's furious at you. You meant the most to him. I guess he's never gotten over being angry that you wouldn't spend more time with him back in school. All the stuff at college must have unbalanced him, and your party was the last straw. I think he became obsessed with you—that's why he spent so much time trying to scare you. And when he suddenly saw his chance for a final revenge, he took it."

Wendy looked thoroughly shaken. "I should have known. I should have known," she said. "I feel as though it's all my fault. Maybe I could have said something to him back then that would have kept this whole thing from happening!"

"There's no way to know if that's true, Wendy," Nancy said. "I think there was something wrong with him—so wrong that nothing you could have done would have made any difference. He needs professional help."

Wendy was biting her lip. "Well, I still should have been more—more sensitive. These past few days have made me think about how obnoxious I've been. When I think of all the bratty things I did . . ." Her voice trailed off.

There was an awkward silence in the room. Nancy was sure everyone else was thinking the same thing she was. Wendy had gotten a lot nicer since this case had started. But if you told her that, it would be just like saying that she *had* been obnoxious before. How could they cheer her up without seeming rude?

Then Celia smiled. "Consider everything forgotten, Wendy," she said. "In fact, let's all just start over—and let's forget about high school this time around."

"That's the best idea I've heard all day," said Wendy.

"Well, I'm glad *that* case is over," Nancy said to Ned as they watched the last of her friends leave. "It's horrible to see someone you've grown up with turn into—into something like that. Poor Patrick."

"It *is* awful," Ned agreed. "But you did the right thing, Nan. Maybe now he'll be able to get the help he needs."

"I hope so," said Nancy.

"And now," Ned suggested, "maybe we can forget this case. We've only got two more days together before school starts for me."

"I know! I can't believe you have to go back so soon! Are you sure you don't mind spending our last evening together at Wendy's?" Wendy had asked Nancy and Ned to come out to dinner with her the night after next as a way of saying thanks. "Because I could always get out of it."

"No! It'll be fun," said Ned. "Now that the case is over, we'll have a great time."

"We'll *need* a great time to tide us over." Nancy sighed, resting her head on his shoulder. "I mean, it'll be weeks before I see you again!"

"Well, we still have forty-eight hours," Ned said. He leaned forward to kiss her. "Let's make the most of them."

Nancy smiled. "That's one of the things I love about you, Ned," she said. "You always use your time wisely."

Nancy's next case:

Carson Drew takes Nancy on a cruise to exotic Rio de Janeiro. Once on board the *Emerald Queen,* a beautiful widow named Nina da Silva seems to attract his attention. The problem is, Nina happens to be Nancy's top suspect in a strange case of stolen gems.

During her investigation someone tries to harm Nancy with a poisonous spider. Then the handsome young cruise director is wounded by a poisonous dart meant for her. Amid the glittering excitement of Carnival, the teen detective is stalked by a phantom hit man—who wants Nancy stopped before she can discover the priceless treasure of the *Emerald Queen* . . . in *THE BLACK WIDOW,* Case #28 in The Nancy Drew Files™.